The Demon Headmaster Strikes Again

'Genetic research!' Dinah looked up sharply. 'Do you think that's what it is? Something that's escaped from the laboratories?'

When the Hunter family are persuaded to move house, Dinah, Lloyd, and Harvey realize that there is something very strange about the new village. And soon Dinah suspects that their old enemy, the Demon Headmaster, is back. This time, he has got control of a research laboratory, and he's planning to take over Nature itself. But to do that, he needs Dinah. And that means she's in terrible danger . . .

The Demon Headmaster Strikes Again is the fourth and latest book about the Demon Headmaster. It is now a BBC television series.

Gillian Cross has been writing for children for many years, and her books have won the Carnegie Medal, the Smarties Book Prize, and the Whitbread Children's Novel Award. She is married with four children, and lives in Warwickshire. Her hobbies include orienteering and playing the piano.

OTHER BOOKS BY GILLIAN CROSS

The Demon Headmaster Series

The Demon Headmaster
The Prime Minister's Brain
The Revenge of the Demon Headmaster
The Demon Headmaster Strikes Again

♠

The Iron Way
Revolt at Ratcliffe's Rags
A Whisper of Lace
The Dark Behind the Curtain
Born of the Sun
On the Edge
Chartbreak
Roscoe's Leap
A Map of Nowhere
Twin and Super-Twin
Wolf
The Great Elephant Chase
New World

The Demon Headmaster Strikes Again

Gillian Cross

Illustrated by Maureen Bradley

Oxford University Press

Oxford Toronto Melbourne

Oxford University Press, Walton Street, Oxford OX2 6DP

Oxford New York
Athens Auckland Bangkok Bogota Bombay
Buenos Aires Calcutta Cape Town Dar es Salaam
Delhi Florence Hong Kong Istanbul Karachi
Kuala Lumpur Madras Madrid Melbourne
Mexico City Nairobi Paris Singapore
Taipei Tokyo Toronto

and associated companies in
Berlin Ibadan

Oxford is a trade mark of Oxford University Press

A CIP catalogue record for this book is available
from the British Library

Cover design: Slatter–Anderson
Cover photography: J.Cat Photography

ISBN 0 19 271453 8

Printed and bound in Great Britain by
Biddles Ltd, Guildford and King's Lynn

Contents

Chapter 1.................................... *A Really Weird Village . . .*

Chapter 2...*The Impossible Photos*

Chapter 3.................................... *A Hard Choice for Dinah*

Chapter 4...*Disaster in the Dark*

Chapter 5.. *Coma*

Chapter 6.................................... *Looking for Evidence*

Chapter 7......................................*'Just a Little Smear . . .'*

Chapter 8... *The Fly*

Chapter 9.................................... *The Creeper Again*

Chapter 10.................................... *Into the BRC!*

Chapter 11.. *Strange Things Growing*

Chapter 12.. *Telephone Treachery*

Chapter 13...*Hatching*

Chapter 14...*Ready for Testing*

Chapter 15....................................*Into the Tunnels*

Chapter 16.. *No Exit*

Chapter 17.................................... *In the Ice House*

Chapter 18.................................*The End of the Experiment?*

Chapter 1

A Really Weird Village . . .

Simon saw them come. The removal van lumbered down the road, followed by a red car, and both of them stopped at the end house. The children got out of the car and stood talking while their parents unlocked the house. Two boys and a girl.

The older boy was about Simon's age, and he looked disgusted. His voice floated up the road.

'This village is weird! There's no one about.'

The other boy groaned. 'Stop *moaning*, Lloyd! We've got to get used to it, however weird it is. Haven't we, Di?'

The girl nodded. 'Harvey's right. Dad's taken the new job, and so this is our home now. However weird it is.'

'Not much of a home.' Lloyd scowled. 'With the rest of SPLAT a hundred miles away.'

Judging by his expression, SPLAT was something really important, but Simon didn't get a chance to guess what, because the children's father called from the front door.

'Let's get on with the unpacking, then!'

Simon watched them run into the house. They might be new, but they'd got one thing right straight away.

It *was* a weird village.

'It's creepy!' Lloyd said. 'There's no one around.'

They'd been unpacking for two days, and it was almost the first break they'd had. Harvey was flopped out on the floor, but Lloyd was by the sitting-room window, gazing moodily out across the village green.

1

Dinah looked at her brothers and thought how different the two of them were. They were both upset about moving, but Harvey was trying to make the best of it. Not like Lloyd. He'd been grumpy and irritable ever since they left their old house.

'It's only a village,' Harvey said soothingly. 'You can't expect a lot of people.'

'You'd get more people on an iceberg in the Arctic,' growled Lloyd. He glared at the post office and the shabby little shop. 'It's *dead*.'

'Well, it's where we live,' Dinah said briskly. She picked up her purse. 'Why don't we go and explore a bit? Mum's nipping out to look at the shops. Let's go too. Maybe we can buy some postcards of the village.'

Harvey jumped up, but Lloyd didn't move.

'Oh, wow!' he said sarcastically. 'What a treat!'

Dinah felt like shaking him. 'You'll never settle in if you don't try to like it.'

'I don't want to settle in. I'm going to stay here and write to the others.'

Harvey stared. 'What for?'

'Because we're still SPLAT!' Lloyd said fiercely. 'The Society for the Protection of our Lives Against Them. Remember? I care about keeping in touch, even if you don't.'

'But they're coming to stay,' Harvey said. 'They'll be here in a couple of days.'

'Exactly!' Lloyd sat down at the table and took out his pen. 'And they need to know what to expect.'

Dinah sighed. Maybe writing to SPLAT would cheer him up, but it didn't seem very likely. As she and Harvey

left the room, she caught sight of the beginning of the letter.

Dear Ian, Mandy and Ingrid,
  This place is a million times worse than I expected . . .

Harvey obviously felt like that about the shops. He stared through the window of the little supermarket and pulled a face. 'Looks really exciting. I don't think.'

Mrs Hunter shrugged. 'You haven't got to come in. Go with Dinah and take a look at the post office.'

Harvey peered through the post office window and three old ladies in woolly hats peered back at him. He shuddered.

'I know,' Dinah said quickly. 'Go down to that bus stop and see when the buses go into town.'

Harvey brightened. 'Now that *is* a good idea. Checking the escape route.'

He ran off, and Mrs Hunter smiled at Dinah. 'Well done. I don't know how I managed before you came to live with us.'

Dinah grinned back and pushed open the post office door. As she walked in, the three old ladies stopped talking and stared. Dinah smiled politely and went up to the counter.

'Hallo. Have you got any postcards of the village?'

The postmistress shook her head. 'There's no call for them,' she said frostily. 'We don't get many visitors.'

There was something unpleasant about the way she said *visitors*. Dinah laughed quickly.

'Oh, I'm not a visitor. We've come to live here. My dad's got a job at the Biogenetic Research Centre. Doing public relations.'

'At the BRC?' All at once, the woman's whole face altered. It was like magic. Her eyes lit up and she gave Dinah a warm, friendly smile. 'The BRC is a wonderful thing to have in the village. It's a really good neighbour.'

'Oh. That's nice.' Dinah blinked, startled by the sudden change.

She was even more startled when she turned round and found the three old ladies muttering behind her.

'. . . wonderful thing, the BRC . . .'

'. . . in the village . . .'

'. . . really good neighbour . . .'

It was all Dinah could do not to shudder. Maybe Lloyd was right when he said the village was creepy.

She bought some stamps and a map of the nearest town, and then went outside to meet Harvey. He was smiling as he came back from the bus stop.

'I've just met the doctor. Doctor Gill. She was really nice. Especially when I told her where Dad was working. She thinks the BRC's a wonderful thing.'

Mrs Hunter was coming out of the supermarket and she smiled when she heard what Harvey said. 'I was rather worried that people might be unfriendly. I thought they might not like the BRC, because it does genetic engineering. But it's obviously very popular. Someone's just been telling me what a good neighbour it is.'

A wonderful thing . . . A really good neighbour . . . It was the same words, all the time. Dinah thought how peculiar it was, but she didn't say anything, because her mother and Harvey were looking so happy. What was the point of upsetting them?

All the same, she was frowning as they walked back across the village green.

They were almost home, when Harvey pointed down the road. 'Isn't that Lloyd? By the post-box. Who's that with him?'

Lloyd was talking to a boy about his own age, and they were both smiling. Dinah grinned.

'Looks as though he's made a friend.'

'Hurrah!' Mrs Hunter said, under her breath.

But she spoke too soon. Lloyd said something—and suddenly the other boy's expression changed. He stopped smiling and backed away quickly, disappearing round the corner.

Lloyd shoved his letter into the post-box and came marching down the road. He looked furious.

'I hate this place! And I hate the BRC! I wish they'd never offered Dad a job!'

'It's not their fault,' said Dinah.

'Oh, *isn't* it?' Lloyd said darkly. 'Didn't you see what just happened?'

'We saw you talking to a boy,' Mrs Hunter said.

'That's right!' said Lloyd. 'His name's Simon, and he was really friendly. Until I mentioned where Dad was working. And then—pow!—he couldn't get away fast enough. People in this village must hate the place.'

'But they don't,' Harvey said. 'They love it. Don't they, Mum?'

Mrs Hunter nodded. 'They seem to.'

'Simon didn't love it!' Lloyd said fiercely. 'If you'd seen his face—'

'He's only one person,' said Harvey. 'We've talked to lots of people. And they all said—'

'Stop it, you two!' Mrs Hunter pushed the front gate open. 'Let's wait for the expert, shall we? Dad's supposed to know exactly what people think of the BRC. It's his job.'

'It's the easiest job I ever had!' Mr Hunter leaned back in the armchair and sipped his tea, smiling at Mrs Hunter. 'I don't need to worry about the village. No one's bothered about the research. They all think the BRC is wonderful. A really good neighbour.'

Dinah felt the back of her neck prickle. She looked round at her mother and Harvey, but they hadn't noticed anything odd. Harvey was thinking about something quite different.

'So what *is* this research?'

'It's to do with DNA,' Mr Hunter said. 'Genes and all that stuff.'

Harvey looked blank. 'What kind of DNA?'

'Any old kind, I think. I saw them taking in a tank full of lizards today, for example. They must be going to do some work with those.'

'What kind of work?' Lloyd said suspiciously.

'Search me.' Mr Hunter reached into his briefcase and pulled out a thick book. 'Why don't you read about it?'

Lloyd leaned over his shoulder and read the title. '*DNA and Evolution. By Professor C. Rowe of the University of Wessex.* No thanks!' He backed away. 'Give it to Di.'

Mr Hunter laughed and held it out. 'Would you like it, Dinah?'

'Really?' Dinah's eyes lit up. 'But don't you need it?'

'Certainly not! I can't plough through all that.' Her father looked horrified.

Dinah took the book. 'Don't you need to understand the research? If you're managing the BRC's public relations?'

Mr Hunter grinned. 'I'm learning the easy way. They're sending me on a course.'

'That's nice,' Mrs Hunter said. She glanced round from the box she was unpacking. 'When does it start?'

'Well, actually . . .' Mr Hunter looked suddenly sheepish. 'I have to leave the day after tomorrow.'

'*The day after tomorrow?*' Mrs Hunter put down the pile of plates she was unwrapping. 'But that's Saturday.'

'I know,' Mr Hunter said, apologetically. 'That's what I said when the Director told me. But I couldn't really argue. You know they offered me this job out of the blue. And they're paying me a fortune. I've got to do something to earn it.'

Lloyd looked furious. 'But we've only just got here.'

'You wouldn't be here at all,' Mr Hunter said, 'if they hadn't lent us this house until we sell our old one.'

Mrs Hunter sighed. 'I suppose you're right. They have treated us very well. I just wish they'd let you stay until I get to know a few people.'

'But you do know someone!' Mr Hunter looked a bit more cheerful. 'Guess who I met at work today!'

Mrs Hunter shook her head. 'I can't imagine.'

'Mrs Carter!' Mr Hunter said triumphantly. 'Remember her? The Director phoned her unexpectedly—just the way he did with me—and offered her a job in the personnel department.'

Mrs Hunter looked vague. 'Mrs Carter?'

'You know. Tall woman with a double chin. Got a daughter called Rose.'

Rose Carter!

Dinah nearly jumped out of her skin. She'd never thought she would hear that name again. Her mind began to fill with pictures.

Rose's blank hypnotized face. Her cold eyes. Her mechanical chanting: *The prefects are the voice of the Head-master. They must be obeyed.* The Demon Headmaster had had their whole school in his power, with everyone hypnotized into obedience—except SPLAT. Rose had been his ideal prefect.

And she was here? In the village?

Dinah glanced at Lloyd and Harvey. She could see that they were stunned too.

'Rose is here?' Mrs Hunter was looking relieved. 'That's nice. I'll ask her round to see the children.'

That was obviously the last straw for Lloyd. A terrible end to a terrible day.

'Come on, Harvey,' he said gruffly. 'I'll give you a game on the computer.'

Dinah wanted to talk about the strange things that were happening, but she could see that Lloyd wasn't in the right mood for that. She would have to wait.

With a sigh, she picked up the book about DNA and evolution, and began to read.

Each living thing has its own, unique DNA, which took millions of years to evolve . . .

She was still reading at bedtime, when Mrs Hunter came in to say goodnight.

'Can't I have a bit longer, Mum? I'll put my own light out.'

'Well . . . all right.' Mrs Hunter smiled. 'After all, you're not going to school at the moment. And it'll be nice for Dad if *one* of us understands what the BRC is up to. Goodnight.'

Dinah mumbled something as her mother went out of the door. She wished she *did* understand what the BRC was up to. Slipping out of bed, she went over to the window and opened it, parting the curtains. With her chin on her hands, she stared across the village at the BRC laboratory.

The whole building was black and shadowy, except for two lights, low down at one end. They glowed through the night like two dull eyes. Could people still be working there, so late?

What were they doing?

Without knowing why, Dinah shuddered. The building looked like a great monster, crouched there in the dark. Like something evil, waiting to pounce.

She was just going to close the curtains, when a noise came drifting towards her, through the night. From the direction of the BRC building.

Bzzz-ZZZ-zzz-ZZZ.

An insect noise? No, it was too loud. And it was too irregular for a machine. What could it be?

BZZZ-zzz-ZZZ-zzz.

Dinah leaned further out of the window, trying to pinpoint exactly where the noise was coming from, but it dwindled and died away. She didn't hear it again, even

though she waited another ten minutes. She climbed back into bed feeling miserable and uneasy. The BRC was definitely peculiar.

Everyone sang its praises—in the same words.

Rose Carter's mother had been offered a job there at exactly the same time as Mr Hunter.

And now there was this mysterious buzzing.

How could she make sense of it all? She felt like racing round the village, asking questions. But would anyone answer? People would just say: *the BRC is a wonderful thing to have in the village . . . a really good neighbour.* She would never find out anything like that.

Unless . . .

The answer came just as she was drifting off to sleep. What about the boy that Lloyd had met? What was his name? Simon. *He* didn't think the BRC was wonderful. Maybe he would tell them what was going on.

If they could get him to talk to them.

Chapter 2

The Impossible Photos

Simon didn't want to talk. Not to anyone connected with the BRC. He'd liked the look of Lloyd—until he heard where his father worked. After that, there didn't seem to be any point in trying to be friends.

So the next day, when Lloyd waved at him from the other side of the village green, he ignored him. That didn't put Lloyd off though. He muttered something to the other boy and the girl who were with him, and all three of them began to walk across the green, heading straight for Simon.

Simon slid off round the corner, but that didn't get rid of Lloyd. Looking back, Simon saw him following. He broke into a run, to get away, but Lloyd started running too.

'Hey! Don't go. I want to talk to you.'

I'm sick of talking to people who don't listen, Simon thought fiercely. He ran faster.

But he hadn't realized how determined the three of them were. The other boy and the girl had gone round the opposite way, past the church. When Simon turned down the alley by the cemetery, there they were—coming to head him off.

'We only want to talk,' the girl said. 'Please.'

Simon spun round, but Lloyd was still behind him.

'We want to ask you about the BRC,' he said.

That was the last thing Simon had expected. He looked at them. The girl had bright, intelligent eyes, and Lloyd and the other boy had friendly grins.

Simon sighed and asked his test question. 'What do you think of the BRC then?'

The BRC is a wonderful thing to have in the village . . . That was the answer he was expecting. But he didn't get it. They just looked back at him, cautiously.

'We think it's . . . odd,' the girl said at last. 'That's why we want to talk to you.'

'You don't think it's a really good neighbour?'

Simon saw the girl's eyes flicker. She'd noticed that everyone used those words, had she? But she didn't have a chance to say so, because Lloyd exploded angrily.

'Why does everyone think the place is so wonderful?'

Simon shrugged. 'I don't know. They never used to. It's only since the meeting.'

'What meeting?' said the other boy.

'There was a public meeting when the new Director arrived at the BRC. About . . .' Simon frowned, trying to remember. 'About six months ago. They booked the village hall, and the Director came to speak. And ever since then, everyone's adored the Research Centre.'

'Must have been some meeting.' Lloyd grinned. 'Whatever did the Director say?'

'I don't know,' Simon said. 'I was . . . doing something else.' He stopped.

But the girl was watching his face. 'It was something important, wasn't it?' she said softly.

'It was important to me,' Simon said gruffly.

'Was it something to do with the BRC?'

How had she guessed that? Simon felt his face go red. 'Might be,' he growled.

He was deliberately trying to be off-putting, but the girl refused to be put off. 'Won't you tell us?'

'I . . .' Simon hesitated. They sounded as if they might listen. *Really* listen, not like his father. He wanted to explain the whole peculiar business, to see what they thought—but he was sick of being called a liar.

'We won't tell anyone else,' Lloyd said. 'Not if it's a secret.'

Simon hesitated again—and then made up his mind. 'All right, I'll tell you. But I'll have to get some things from home first.'

'Lead on,' said Lloyd.

They went up the lane to Simon's house. He stopped outside, with his hand on the broken gate.

'Hang on out here while I get them. Then we can go round to your house.'

They thought that was odd, he could see. But he never invited people in. Not if his father was there. Leaving them by the gate, he hurried indoors to get the pictures.

Ten minutes later, they were in the Hunters' sitting-room.

'Bit of a mess, I'm afraid,' Lloyd said apologetically.

Simon almost laughed. Didn't they know how lucky they were? They might not have finished unpacking, but the house was warm and friendly, and their mother had smiled when they walked in. His house had been like that too, before his mother died.

He sat down and took the photos out of his pocket.

'What are those?' Lloyd said. 'Something to do with why you missed that meeting?'

Simon nodded. 'I was trying to photograph some badgers.'

Dinah looked delighted. 'Are there badgers round here?'

'In the woods behind the BRC,' said Simon. 'I'd been trying to get some photographs for ages, but they were too nervous when I was around. And the flash scared them off.'

'So what did you do?' Harvey said.

Simon grinned suddenly. He'd been really pleased with his plan. 'I worked out how to take the photographs without being there. I'd been watching them with a red lamp, because red light doesn't disturb them. So I bought some infra-red film, and rigged up a time switch. To get the camera to take pictures automatically, every twenty minutes.'

'That was why you missed the meeting?' Lloyd said. 'Because you were setting it all up?'

Simon nodded. 'I didn't think it would matter. I thought Dad or someone would tell me about the meeting. But no one would say anything afterwards, except how wonderful the BRC was.'

Harvey's eyes went to the envelope. 'And what about the photographs?'

Simon took the pictures out and laid them on the table, in a row. There were ten of them. Harvey gave a cry of delight.

'*Baby* badgers!'

Simon smiled and waited.

It was Dinah who spotted the creeper. She leaned forward suddenly, catching her breath.

'What is it?'

'What's what?' Lloyd said.

Dinah pointed at the first picture. Not at the badgers, but at the bare wall behind them. Then she ran her finger along the row of photographs, pointing at the wall in each one.

In the third picture, the creeper just showed above the
top. A couple of tiny leaves at the end of a shoot.

By the fifth picture, that shoot was looping over the wall
and down the other side.

And by the tenth picture, it was snaking across the
ground, towards the camera. A vigorous, twisting stem
with leaves sprouting all the way along it.

'It grew that much?' Dinah said. 'In less than three hours?'
Lloyd and Harvey stared.

'It's impossible,' Lloyd said. 'Nothing grows that fast.'

'That creeper did.' Simon watched their faces, waiting to see if they believed him. Wondering if they really understood how peculiar it was. 'It was heading for the light.'

Dinah realized what he was saying. 'But it was a *red* light. Plants don't react to that.'

'Normal plants don't.' Simon began to gather up the pictures. 'But maybe this isn't a normal plant.'

'Not normal?' Harvey shivered. 'What is it, then?'

Dinah held out her hand. 'May I have another look?' Simon handed over the pictures and she flicked through them, frowning. 'I've never seen a plant like that.'

'It might be a completely new plant,' Simon said. As casually as he could manage. 'That wall is the wall behind the BRC. Where they do—'

'Genetic research!' Dinah looked up sharply. 'Do you think that's what it is? Something that's escaped from the laboratories?'

'Could be,' Simon said cautiously. 'It's very—'

And then the door bell rang.

Mrs Hunter called down the hall. 'You've got another visitor!'

'Now?' Lloyd muttered crossly. 'Who on earth—?'

'Why don't we go and see?' Dinah looked apologetically at Simon. 'We won't be a minute.'

She walked into the hall, still holding the photographs. But it was Lloyd who saw the visitor first. He came past Dinah and stopped dead.

'Rose Carter!'

Dinah thought she'd never heard anyone sound so unwelcoming, but Rose didn't seem to mind. She stood on the doorstep, looking just the same as ever. Smooth and secretive and self-satisfied.

'What are you doing here?' Harvey said at last.

Rose smiled smugly at Mrs Hunter. 'I was invited.'

'That's right.' Mrs Hunter smiled back. 'I thought you'd like to catch up with each other's news. Bring her in, Lloyd, and I'll leave you to it.'

She walked back down the hall, into the study, and Rose stepped in and shut the front door.

'Why are you all staring?' she said.

Harvey gritted his teeth. 'You know why!'

Lloyd nodded and began to chant. '*All pupils shall obey the prefects.*'

'Oh, that!' Rose laughed brightly. 'That was ages ago!'

She hadn't altered. Not a bit. Dinah stared at her.

Grimly Lloyd went on with his chant. '*The prefects are the voice of the Headmaster.*'

It looked as though Rose was going to ignore him. But as he reached the last word, an extraordinary change came over her face. The moment he said the word *Headmaster*, her mouth twisted, as if she were going to be sick. She gave a huge shudder.

'The Headmaster was a horrible man!' she said fiercely. 'Don't talk about him!'

They blinked at her.

'Could you . . . er . . . repeat that?' Lloyd said.

Rose looked baffled. 'Repeat what?'

'About the Headmaster.'

Dinah couldn't believe it was going to happen again. But it did. Rose's mouth twisted in exactly the same way, and she gave another shudder. 'The Headmaster was a horrible man! Don't talk about him!'

For a moment, no one spoke. Then Harvey said slowly, 'You've changed your mind.'

Rose nodded. 'Of course.'

Lloyd gave her a long, hard look. 'You do seem . . . different.'

'I am different,' Rose said smoothly. 'I want to be friends. You're the only people I know in this village.' She held out her hand.

Somewhere at the back of Dinah's mind a warning bell rang, very faintly. But Lloyd was already smiling. He grasped Rose's hand and shook it, hard.

'No point in holding grudges. Yes, let's be friends. We could do with another friend in this village.'

Harvey nodded. 'It's a weird place, isn't it? Know what we've just found out?' He stopped and looked at Lloyd. 'Can I tell her?'

No! thought Dinah. But Lloyd reached over and twitched Simon's photographs out of her hands.

'Take a look at these, Rose,' he said. 'They were taken twenty minutes apart. On an automatic switch.'

Slowly, Rose fanned the pictures out in her hand. Harvey leaned over her shoulder and pointed, helpfully.

'That's the back wall of the BRC. And look what's growing over it!'

Rose's eyes flickered. 'Where did you get these?'

'From a boy in the village,' Lloyd said. 'Come and meet

him.' He backed down the hall and flung open the sitting-room door. 'Simon, this is—'

Then he stopped. They all stared into the room.

'Where is he?' Harvey said. 'He's vanished.'

Rose raised one eyebrow. 'Run away, maybe.'

'Mum!' Lloyd went across the hall. 'Do you know where Simon is?'

Mrs Hunter looked up from her boxes in the study. 'Someone went out of the back door. Was that him?'

'I suppose so.' Lloyd went back into the sitting-room, frowning.

'He's gone?' Harvey said.

'Looks like it.'

Rose gave a small, prim smile. 'I expect he lost his nerve,' she purred.

'What do you mean?' Dinah said sharply.

'Well, you don't think these are genuine, do you?' Rose waved the photographs with a scornful smile.

'Why shouldn't they be?' Lloyd snapped. He hated being fooled.

'Oh, come *on*. It's obvious.'

'I don't see why.' Dinah took the pictures out of Rose's hand. 'They look real enough to me.'

Rose just smirked. 'Why are there only ten of them, then? What happened to the rest of the film?'

Harvey's face fell. 'That's a point.'

Lloyd hesitated. 'But how could you fake photographs like that?'

'He might have taken them on different days,' Rose said. 'Weeks apart, maybe.'

Lloyd and Harvey looked at each other. They were

20

obviously changing their minds. Dinah felt like shaking them.

'Don't you think we ought to ask Simon about that? And give him a chance to explain?'

Rose looked at her, pityingly. 'If he's told one lie, he'll just tell another one, won't he?'

Dinah opened her mouth to argue, but Rose didn't give her time. She went straight on, in a superior, patronizing voice.

'You don't find it easy, do you? Admitting you're wrong.'

'It's not like that!' Dinah said angrily.

But Lloyd was getting impatient. 'Who cares about some boring old plant, anyway? Let's go and play a computer game or something.'

Rose smiled triumphantly. 'That would be lovely. I'm good at computer games. Where is the computer?'

'Upstairs.' Lloyd led the way, and Rose and Harvey followed him.

But Dinah didn't. She couldn't bear any more of Rose. She let them go and when they were safely shut in with the computer, she slipped out of the front door.

And headed for Simon's house.

Chapter 3

A Hard Choice for Dinah

Simon was lying on his bed, staring miserably into his worm tank. Watching the worms churn up the different layers of earth.

He'd run away. He'd even left his pictures behind. How could he have been so feeble? Just because he'd thought Lloyd sounded annoyed when he said *Rose Carter*. He was probably completely wrong about that, anyway. Probably Rose was a good friend of theirs. They'd all be telling her about him—and laughing.

He was so angry with himself that he didn't take any notice when the doorbell rang downstairs. He waited for his father to haul himself out of the armchair. What did it matter who it was? They never had any real visitors, anyway. Not now.

The knock on his bedroom door took him by surprise. He was even more surprised when he opened the door and found Dinah standing outside.

'I brought your pictures back . . .' she began, rather stiffly. Then she glanced over his shoulder, and her face changed. 'What a lovely room!'

'Do you like it?' Simon said.

He stepped back to let her in and she walked round, staring. At the animal posters. And the worm tank. And the formicarium.

'You've got a wasps' nest as well! How *beautiful!*'

Simon looked up at the fragile, irregular ball of wasp paper, honeycombed with tunnels. He thought it was beautiful too. He'd always wanted one, ever since his mother had told him about wasps chewing rotten wood to build their nests.

'You're the first person who's ever recognized it. Are you interested in nature?'

'I'm interested in all kinds of science. I like to understand things. That's why—' Dinah stopped.

'You want to understand why I ran off?'

She nodded unhappily. 'Rose said you lost your nerve. Because you'd faked the photographs.'

'Everyone thinks I faked them,' Simon said bitterly. He took the pictures out of Dinah's hand. 'Never mind. Thanks for bringing them back, anyway.'

He thought she would go, and he turned his back to make it easy for her to leave without being embarrassed. But she didn't move. When he looked round again, she was staring at him.

'I don't think they're fakes,' she said steadily. 'You don't seem like a faker to me.'

Simon swallowed. 'You believe me?'

'I think so. But . . .' Dinah hesitated.

'Yes? Go on.'

'Well . . . why are there only ten pictures? What happened to the rest of the film?'

'I'll show you what happened!' Simon said fiercely. 'It was ruined. Because the camera was destroyed!'

Dropping to his knees, he felt under his bed for the squashed scarred plastic. Pulling it out, he dropped it into Dinah's hands.

'Look! What do you think of that?'

Dinah was stunned. She turned the camera over and over, running her fingers across the jagged cracks and the strange,

regular scars. It seemed as if something had stuck to the surface of the plastic and been pulled off.

When she looked up, she saw Simon watching her. Waiting for her reaction.

'How did it get like this?' she said softly.

'The creeper. When I went back in the morning, there were shoots tangled all round the camera. They crushed it and ruined the second half of the film.'

Dinah studied the scars again. 'Where is the creeper? Have you got any of it?'

Simon shook his head. 'It was all withered. I should have brought some back, shouldn't I? But I didn't realize what had happened until the film was developed. I just thought—' He stopped.

'Yes?' Dinah said.

Simon looked down at his hands. 'I thought the security guards had found it.'

'*Security guards?*'

'From the BRC. Since the new Director came, they've guarded the place like a fortress.'

Dinah was very quiet for a moment. Then she said, 'If they've got a plant like that, and it's escaping—people ought to know.'

'You think I haven't tried to tell everyone?' Simon said. 'No one will listen.'

Dinah looked at the camera again. 'Maybe you need to get a new camera and take some more pictures. With a witness.'

'Are you offering to come?'

'I'd like to know what's going on,' Dinah said slowly. She ran a finger over the strange scars on the plastic. 'Maybe Lloyd and Harvey would come too. Then you'd have three witnesses.'

Simon looked eagerly at her. 'How about tomorrow night? I was going to buy a new camera anyway, with my birthday money. If I go into town tomorrow, I can get it in time.'

Dinah took a deep breath. Then she nodded. 'I'll go straight home and ask them!'

She ran all the way home. She could hear Lloyd and Harvey talking in Lloyd's bedroom, and she raced straight upstairs.

'I've been to see Simon, and he showed me—'

Then she saw Rose, sitting at the computer.

'Back again?' Rose purred. 'How was Simon then? Did you get him to tell the truth?'

'He *was* telling the truth!' Dinah said.

Rose looked triumphantly at Lloyd and Harvey. 'You see? I said she couldn't cope with changing her mind.'

They shuffled their feet and looked uneasy. Dinah stared. What had Rose been saying, while she was at Simon's?

She tried not to sound annoyed. 'I asked Simon why there were only ten pictures and it's because the creeper grew right round the camera. The shoots cracked it right open. I saw it!'

Rose gave a very small snigger.

Dinah tried to ignore her, but Lloyd and Harvey had heard the snigger and they looked away awkwardly. There was an uncomfortable silence.

Then Lloyd said, 'It's all pretty hard to believe.'

'That doesn't mean it's not true,' Dinah said. 'You've got to look at the evidence.'

'Evidence?' Harvey's eyes lit up. 'Like what?'

'Well, there's the pictures,' Dinah began. 'And the camera.' She saw Rose smirking, but she wasn't going to be put off. 'And the village is weird, isn't it? People keep saying the same things about the BRC. Doesn't that remind you—'

Doesn't that remind you of school? she was going to say. *When the Headmaster was there.* But Rose interrupted her.

'Grown-ups always say the same things. Listen. Here's your mum coming upstairs. I bet she'll say, "It's getting dark, Rose. You'd better go home before your mother starts worrying".'

Lloyd and Harvey turned towards the door. Their mother pushed it open, smiling.

'It's getting rather late, Rose dear. Do you think you ought to go home? Before your mother starts worrying about you being out in the dark?'

'Of course,' Rose said smoothly.

She didn't say anything else. She didn't need to. She just looked triumphantly at Dinah as Mrs Hunter went downstairs.

'That's not the same at all!' Dinah protested. 'Mum didn't use exactly the words you said—'

Rose shook her head with a taunting smile. 'Can't admit you're wrong, can you? Look at the evidence, Dinah Hunter.' She headed for the door, waving a hand at the boys. 'Thanks for the game. See you again soon.'

The moment she was outside, Dinah caught hold of Lloyd's arm. 'I *am* going to look at the evidence!' she said. 'Simon and I are going round to the back of the BRC tomorrow night. To look for some of that creeper. Come with us!'

'It's just another trick,' Lloyd growled.

'No it's not!'

Harvey tried to calm things down. 'Why don't we wait a couple of days? The rest of SPLAT will be here then. We can investigate with them.'

Lloyd jumped at the excuse. 'That'll be much better. Wait for the others, Di. Don't go with Simon.'

Dinah wished she could agree. She hated quarrelling. But she remembered the look on Simon's face when he found that she believed him. She couldn't let him down now.

27

'I've got to go tomorrow night. I promised Simon.'

Lloyd lost his temper. 'Simon, Simon, *Simon*! You can't stop talking about him, can you? Go off investigating tomorrow night, then, if you'd rather go with him. But don't expect us to come!'

Dinah bit her lip. But all she said was, 'I've got to keep my promise.'

The next day was miserable anyway, because it was Saturday, and Mr Hunter left for his course. When they waved him off after breakfast, the house seemed empty and lonely.

By the evening, Lloyd was in a really bad temper. He went to bed early, shutting his door firmly behind him.

Harvey followed Dinah into her room. 'Will you be all right?' he whispered unhappily. 'I mean . . . if you want me to come . . .'

Dinah was tempted. She didn't really fancy sneaking out on her own. But if Harvey went, Lloyd would be furious and there would be a terrible row. Then Harvey would be even more unhappy. She reached over and squeezed his hand.

'Thanks. But it's all right. I'll go on my own, and tell you about it in the morning.'

Harvey grinned, and she knew that he was relieved. 'OK. But beware of the Killer Creeper!'

He went off to his own room, and Dinah began to sort out some warm clothes. She was going to hide them under her pillow, and put them on after Mrs Hunter had been in to say goodnight. Then all she had to do was stay awake until midnight, to sneak out and meet Simon. She wasn't looking forward to it.

And Harvey's joke about the Killer Creeper hadn't helped.

Lloyd was woken in the pitch dark, by a hand that clutched at his arm.

'She's gone!'

'What?' He rubbed his eyes and looked at his watch. 'Are you mad, Harvey? It's midnight.'

'Of course it is. And Dinah's gone out. On her own.'

'She won't be on her own for long,' Lloyd said crossly. 'She'll be with Simon.'

'Yes, but—' Harvey sat down on the bed. 'We don't really know him, do we? If he faked those pictures, he might be a maniac. Do you think we ought to tell Mum?'

'Don't be an idiot.' Lloyd could just imagine how their mother would react if they told her they'd let Dinah go out at night. On her own. 'Do you want to be boiled in oil?'

'Then I'm going to follow Di!' Harvey said.

Lloyd groaned and sat up. 'You're not serious?'

'She's our *sister*. I'm going after her, even if you're not.'

Lloyd closed his eyes for a moment, wishing he were still asleep. Then he groaned again and swung his legs out of bed. 'I'll go. You stay here.' He began to tug on a sweatshirt over his pyjamas.

'I'm not scared!' Harvey whispered fiercely.

'Of course you're not.' Lloyd picked up his jeans. 'But it's cold out there, and you're the one with the weak chest. Stay here—and send out a search party if we all get eaten by the dreaded creeper. Now go back to bed, and stop worrying.'

A couple of minutes later, Lloyd was inching down the stairs, with his shoes in one hand and a torch in the other.

Chapter 4

Disaster in the Dark

Simon had only been waiting a couple of minutes when he saw Dinah running up the lane. He peered into the shadows behind her, trying to see if Lloyd and Harvey had come too. For a moment he thought he glimpsed another figure. Then it seemed to melt into the bushes.

'Hallo?' he called softly.

'Hi,' Dinah panted.

'On your own?'

'Yes.'

Dinah's voice was tight. Simon guessed she'd been having problems, but he could hear that she didn't want to talk about them.

'Come on then,' he said briskly. 'It's this way. Up past the BRC and round into the woods at the back.'

The BRC building was a big old house on the edge of the village. There were security lights all round the main entrance, but the building itself was dark. Except for a light in one window, on the ground floor.

Dinah looked at it curiously. 'Someone's still working?'

'There's always people working late.' Simon shrugged. 'It was like that even when my mum started there, years ago. And it's got worse since the new Director came.'

'Your mum works at the BRC?'

'She used to. She's dead now.' Simon began to walk faster. He didn't want to talk about his mother.

The side wall of the building ran along the lane. It was blank and windowless, and it joined straight on to the long garden wall. When they reached the corner, at the end of the garden, Simon turned off the road, into the woods. It was dark under the trees and Dinah turned on her torch.

Simon waved his, apologetically. 'This won't be much use. It's the red one.'

'Turn it on anyway,' Dinah said. 'After all, that's the one the creeper was heading for.'

Simon flicked the switch and shone the red light up at the back wall of the garden. 'No sign of any creeper there now.'

'Where was it before?'

'Up by the badger sett. Let's take a look.' Simon began to work his way through the trees.

They were almost half-way to the sett, when a twig cracked, a long way behind. Dinah looked round sharply.

'What's the matter?' Simon said.

'It's just—oh, it's silly really, but I had a funny feeling before, when I was coming to meet you. As if there were someone following me.'

Dinah shone her torch back into the woods, but there was nothing to be seen except trees and brambles. After a moment, Simon shrugged.

'Don't let's waste time. The badger sett's over there, by that big tree.'

Dinah looked. 'What are we going to do?'

'I thought we could sit under the tree, where the camera was before. With the red light on.'

'As long as we don't land up like the camera,' Dinah said lightly. 'I don't want to be squashed to bits.'

It sounded like a joke, but Simon could tell that she was nervous. 'We'll be fine,' he said. 'Let's sit under the tree.'

They settled themselves on the carpet of dry leaves, leaning back against the trunk.

'Turn your torch off,' Simon whispered. 'In case the security guards see it. We just need the red one.'

With Dinah's torch switched off, the wood seemed more threatening. Leaves rustled round them, and there were odd squeaks and grunts.

And then another twig snapped.

Simon caught his breath. 'Do you think we're really being followed?'

'Who would follow us?' whispered Dinah.

'The guards, of course.' Simon turned off the red torch as well. 'Sssh.'

They huddled under the tree, in the dark. There was a

rustle, and the sound of something brushing against a branch. Then a faint light shone out of the bushes.

Torch light.

They didn't dare to move. Sitting under the tree, they watched the torch beam flick quickly backwards and forwards, as if it were searching for someone. Simon tried to keep calm. After all, they had a perfect right to be in the woods. But he didn't fancy tangling with the BRC security guards.

The beam of light swung round towards the wall. Simon was expecting it to sweep back again, straight at their hiding place under the tree. But it didn't. It stayed pointing at the wall. And the footsteps began to move away in that direction.

Then there was a scrabbling sound.

'He's climbing the wall,' whispered Dinah. 'Whatever for?'

Before they could work it out, they heard a completely different noise.

Bzzz-ZZZ-zzz-ZZZ.

'That sound!' Dinah grabbed Simon's arm. 'I've heard it before!'

Simon nodded. 'So have I. But never so close. What is it?'

'I don't know.' Dinah stood up and switched her torch on, shining it towards the wall.

Bzzz-ZZZ-zzz-ZZZ.

For a second, they both saw a startling picture. There was a shadowy figure sitting astride the wall.

Simon frowned. 'Bit small for a guard, isn't he?'

Dinah didn't answer. Instead, she clutched at his arm.

'Look behind!'

Simon looked, and gasped. All along the wall behind the dark figure were long, waving shoots of creeper.

'It wasn't there before!' hissed Dinah. 'It's grown since we walked past. And the buzzing—'

The buzzing was getting louder, but they never saw what was making it, because their voices must have carried further than they thought. The person on the wall suddenly swung his torch round and it shone straight into their eyes, blinding them.

'It *is* a security guard!' hissed Simon. 'RUN!'

They started scrambling back through the trees and there was a yell from behind.

'Hey! Wait!'

'Don't stop!' Simon panted.

While he was speaking, there was another burst of angry buzzing.

BZZZ-ZZZ-ZZZ-ZZZ!

Then a long rustle, followed by a thud.

'He's jumped off the wall,' Dinah panted. 'Must be . . . coming . . . after us. Shouldn't we . . . stop and explain?'

Simon didn't answer. He just kept running. He didn't slow down until they were safely in the middle of the village.

'No point in asking for trouble,' he muttered, as soon as he'd got his breath back. 'It's much better to get away. Those guards can be really nasty.'

'But why?' Dinah said. 'What are they guarding?' She looked at Simon, and he saw that she was really worried. 'What do you think is going on?'

Dinah meant to think about it all when she got home. But she was so tired that she fell asleep as soon as she crept into bed. She didn't wake up again until the morning.

When Harvey shook her.

He bent over the bed, shaking her shoulders desperately. 'Wake up, Di! Wake up! Where is he?'

'What's the matter?' Dinah lifted her head sleepily. 'Where's who?'

'Where's Lloyd? He's gone! What's happened to him?'

'How should I know?' It sounded like nonsense, but Harvey looked frantic. Dinah sat up. 'What are you talking about?'

Harvey shook her shoulders again. 'Lloyd followed you last night, to make sure you were OK. And he hasn't come back.'

Suddenly, Dinah was very, very wide awake. 'He can't have followed me. I didn't see him.'

'Do you think he'd let you see?' Harvey looked impatient. 'That would have been like giving in. He was just going to creep along behind you.'

Dinah's throat went dry. She remembered the cracking twigs that she and Simon had heard. Suppose that had been Lloyd?

'What happened?' Harvey said.

Dinah frowned. 'Nothing happened. Except that we saw the creeper, and a guard shone his torch—'

And then she remembered what Simon had said. *Bit small for a guard, isn't he?*

Of course! Why hadn't she listened? It wasn't a guard they'd seen on the wall. It was Lloyd. He must have noticed the creeper and climbed up to investigate. And then—

She closed her eyes, remembering the yell, and that thud. And she felt sick.

Harvey was watching her. 'Tell me,' he said, in a small, scared voice. 'What happened?'

'I don't know what happened,' Dinah muttered. 'But I know where Lloyd was. I'd better go and see if he's still there.'

'Now?'

'Straight away.'

She pulled on the nearest clothes and ran downstairs, with Harvey close behind. Mrs Hunter stuck her head over the banisters.

'Harvey? Dinah? You're not going out, are you?'

'Just for a walk,' Dinah said quickly. She didn't want to worry her mother unnecessarily. Especially when her father wasn't there. 'We won't be long.'

'But your breakfast!'

'We'll have it when we get back. Bye!'

Racing through the front door, Dinah slammed it behind them and began to run up the lane. It seemed much longer than the night before.

'Hang on!' panted Harvey.

'Sorry.' She slowed down, to let him get his breath back, but it was difficult. She kept imagining Lloyd lying out all night, in the cold air. Maybe injured. Maybe unconscious. Wherever he was, there must be something wrong with him, or he would have come home.

When they reached the wood, she swung off the road. The whole place looked quite different in the daylight, but she spotted the tracks that she and Simon had left the night before. It was easy to follow those to the tree where they'd been sitting. When she reached it, she stopped, with one hand on the trunk.

'This is where we were. And someone climbed up on the wall over there.' She pointed.

Harvey looked at her. 'Someone?'

'It was Lloyd. I'm sure it was.'

'So where is he?'

Dinah swallowed. 'There was a yell. And a thump, like someone falling.'

She and Harvey looked at each other.

'Come on,' Harvey said, harshly. 'Let's go and see.'

There was a tree growing against the wall. Underneath it, there were footprints in the mud. And there was one footprint on the wall itself.

'This is where he went up,' Dinah said. 'And look— there's a branch broken off the tree, higher up. He must have pulled it off when he fell.'

'So where is he?' Harvey said.

Dinah swallowed. 'He must be over the other side of the wall. In the garden. Give me a leg up.'

She scrabbled up the wall and stuck her head over the top. There was a tangle of small rhododendron bushes on the other side, and one of them was broken and squashed, as if something heavy had fallen on top of it.

But there was no sign of Lloyd.

Chapter 5

Coma

'Let me get this straight,' Mrs Hunter said weakly. 'You went out at *night*? On your *own*?'

Miserably, Dinah nodded.

'And Lloyd followed you?'

Dinah looked at Harvey, and he nodded too.

Mrs Hunter sat down suddenly at the kitchen table, as if her legs wouldn't hold her up any longer. 'I thought you'd all got more sense. Didn't you *notice* there was someone behind you, Dinah?'

'Well . . . sort of.' Dinah hung her head. 'We kept hearing noises, but we thought it was because we were nervous. In the dark.'

'And then they saw a security guard sitting on top of the wall,' Harvey broke in. 'So they ran away. Only it wasn't a security guard. It was Lloyd. And he fell off. And—'

His voice died away, and he and Dinah looked down at the floor.

'So *where is he*?' Mrs Hunter said.

Dinah and Harvey shook their heads.

Mrs Hunter put her face in her hands and took a long breath. Then she stood up. 'Let's start looking, then. And we'd better phone the police—'

She was interrupted by a knock on the back door. Rose opened it, and stuck her head round.

'Good morning,' she said.

Mrs Hunter managed a faint smile. 'I'm afraid we're rather busy just now, Rose dear. We really haven't got time to talk. Unless—' Her eyes lit up suddenly. '*You* haven't seen Lloyd, have you?'

'Lloyd?' Rose said lightly.

'He went out last night,' muttered Harvey. 'And he hasn't come back.'

Rose frowned. Then, suddenly—almost dramatically—she clapped a hand to her forehead. 'Hang on! What was he wearing?'

Her voice sounded odd to Dinah, but Harvey looked up eagerly.

'Blue jeans and a green sweatshirt. Why?'

'I think I've seen him!' Rose said, with a flourish. 'I've just walked past the old quarry, and there was someone huddled up on the far side. At the bottom of the cliff. I didn't look too closely, because I thought it was some horrible smelly tramp. But I'm sure he was wearing . . . blue jeans and a green sweatshirt!'

Mrs Hunter was half-way to the door before Rose had finished speaking. 'We've got to get up there! Harvey—you stay here and phone an ambulance. Tell it to come straight to the quarry. The rest of us will go on ahead.' She ran out to the car, with Rose at her heels.

Dinah followed, feeling horribly uneasy. It was all too much of a coincidence. Why had Rose walked in at that precise moment? Almost as though she'd *known*? What was going on?

But it wasn't the right moment for questions. They piled into the car and Mrs Hunter started the engine and roared out of the garage. They were at the quarry in five minutes and she drove straight in through the gates, stopping in a patch of sticky mud.

'Where is he?' she said wildly.

Rose opened the door and stepped out delicately. There were fresh tyre tracks all over the mud. 'I think . . .'

For a second, Dinah thought that she didn't know quite where to look. Then her face brightened and she pointed.

'Over there!'

On the far side of the quarry, hardly visible from the road, was a small, huddled figure. Dinah felt even more uneasy. *She can't have seen him from the road. Not if she was just walking past.*

But it was Lloyd all right. He was lying flopped in a heap, as though someone had dropped him there. Mrs Hunter raced across and knelt down, feeling for his pulse. He didn't stir, but she stopped frowning and gave a great shout.

'He's not dead! He's alive!'

Dinah forgot all about Rose. She ran over and knelt beside her mother, staring down at Lloyd. He might be alive, but he wasn't conscious. Dinah shook his shoulder, gently, but he didn't react at all and when she lifted his arm, his hand hung limp.

There was something tangled round his fingers. Dinah unwound it. It was withered and turning brown, and she was just going to toss it away when she suddenly recognized the shape of the leaves. The shock of it made her feel sick. They were just like the leaves in Simon's photos of the creeper.

Mrs Hunter was patting frantically at Lloyd's cheek, trying to wake him up. Trying to stay calm, Dinah bent over and examined his hand. He must have caught hold of the creeper when it was alive, because his palm was covered with little marks from the suckers. Just like Simon's broken camera.

'Mum,' she said. 'Look at this.'

Mrs Hunter glanced vaguely at the creeper, as though she couldn't take in what Dinah was talking about.

'It's a funny time to be thinking about nature study,' murmured Rose. She was standing just behind them. 'I thought you'd be worrying about Lloyd.'

Of course I'm worrying about Lloyd! Dinah wanted to shout.

That's why I want to know what the creeper's doing here! But she didn't want to upset her mother by quarrelling with Rose. Quietly, she pushed the creeper into her pocket and looked round.

Where had it come from? She couldn't see any in the quarry. And Simon seemed to think that it didn't grow anywhere except at the BRC. If that was right, Lloyd *must* have been there. He *must* have been the person sitting on the wall.

So what was he doing here?

She looked down again. Mrs Hunter was wiping the dust off Lloyd's face with her handkerchief. His cheek twitched slightly, but that was the only reaction. He was totally unconscious.

Dinah pushed a hand into her pocket, feeling the dry leaves of the creeper. Then she glanced over her shoulder, at the tyre tracks in the mud beside their car.

That was how he'd got here. Someone had brought him. It was the only explanation that made sense. That weird buzzing had startled him into falling off the wall. And he'd been brought here to stop people asking questions about the BRC.

Dinah shivered. What sort of secret took that much guarding?

And what was wrong with Lloyd?

'Some kind of massive physical shock,' the doctor said.

They all stared down at the unconscious figure in the hospital bed. He looked calm and peaceful and very, very remote. Tubes and wires looped away from his body, connecting him up to the drips and monitors round the bed.

'Is he going to get better?' Mrs Hunter said hesitantly.

'Well, he's not getting any *worse*,' the doctor said. He sounded cautious.

'You don't think . . .' Mrs Hunter swallowed. 'Suppose he fell down into the quarry and hit his head? Is his brain—?'

'Much too early to be worrying about brain damage,' said the doctor briskly.

Dinah thought he sounded a bit too brisk. Mrs Hunter obviously agreed. She closed her eyes for a moment.

'Is there somewhere I can phone my husband from? He's away on a course. I'd better get him to come back.'

The doctor put a hand on her shoulder. 'It might be a good idea to get hold of him. But tell him not to panic. There's no immediate danger.'

'But what's going to happen?' Harvey was looking horrified. They'd picked him up on the way to the hospital, and it was the first time he'd seen the state Lloyd was in. 'Is he going to stay unconscious like this?'

'We just don't know,' the doctor said, reluctantly. 'This is a very odd case. If we knew what *sort* of shock he'd had, that might help.'

Rather nervously, Dinah pulled the creeper out of her pocket. She hadn't said anything so far, but this seemed the right moment. 'He was holding this when we found him. Do you think there could be any connection?'

The doctor looked almost amused. 'I don't think touching a plant would give anyone a shock. Not like the one your brother's had.'

'It did mark the palm of his hand,' Dinah said quickly. 'It's not an ordinary plant.'

The doctor glanced at the marks on Lloyd's hand. 'He wouldn't get those from a plant. And anyway, they're not serious. The skin's not even broken. The only real wound is that puncture in his arm.'

He pulled back the sleeve of Lloyd's gown and took another look at the wound. It was small but deep. As though something the size of a pencil had been stuck straight into the flesh. The skin round it was red and slightly swollen.

'He must have caught himself on a tree when he fell,' the doctor muttered. 'And been spiked by a branch.'

'But there aren't any trees at the quarry—' Dinah began.

Mrs Hunter sighed. 'I think you'd better leave it to the doctors, Dinah dear. They know what they're doing.'

But they don't know, Dinah thought. *That's just what the doctor's saying. They haven't got a clue.* Then she looked at her mother's face and knew that she couldn't go on arguing. Mrs Hunter had enough to worry about.

Dinah pushed the creeper back into her pocket. It was no good showing it to people. Not if they didn't already know how peculiar it was. She needed to talk to someone who understood.

Simon.

He knew there was something weird going on. He would listen to her.

Dinah looked at the drip above Lloyd's head, and the monitor that showed his heartbeat. Then she looked down at his white face on the pillow. *I'll find out what's going on,* she promised silently. *I'll find out how to make you better.*

Chapter 6

Looking for Evidence

As soon as Simon saw Dinah, he knew something terrible had happened. Her face was white, and she looked ready to blurt everything out at once, right there on his doorstep.

'Let's go upstairs,' he said quickly.

'And don't go playing lots of loud records,' his father grunted from the armchair.

Simon glared at him and led the way upstairs. The moment the door was shut, he turned to face Dinah.

'What's the matter?'

'It's Lloyd. He followed us last night. He was in the woods. That crash—'

'That was *him*?' Simon's eyes widened. Then he remembered the size of the figure on the wall and he nodded. 'Yes, that makes sense. What did he say? Did he see what was making that buzzing noise?'

'You don't understand.' Dinah gulped. 'No one knows *what* he saw, because . . . he didn't come back. We found him in the quarry this morning. Unconscious. And he's still unconscious—'

'Is he hurt? Badly?'

'I don't know!' Dinah wailed. 'The doctors can't work out what happened to him. And no one will believe me when I say he was at the BRC. Up on that wall.'

'Hang on a minute.' Simon sat down on the bed, trying to fit everything together. 'You found him at the quarry, and he's still unconscious. Yes? So what makes you think it *was* him on the wall?'

'Because Harvey says he followed us. And this was in his hand when we found him.' Dinah pulled something out of her pocket and dropped it into Simon's lap.

A long trail of brown, withered creeper.

Simon picked it up and turned it over in his hands, but he didn't need to look for long. He recognized it straight away.

'Lloyd was holding this?'

Dinah nodded. 'And there wasn't any growing in the quarry. I looked all round.'

'I bet there wasn't.' Simon knew the quarry as well as he knew his own bedroom. It was his favourite place for bird-watching. 'I've never seen that creeper anywhere. Except behind the Research Centre.'

'It *was* Lloyd on the wall,' Dinah said firmly. 'I went there with Harvey this morning and looked over the top. And there were broken bushes on the other side, where he fell. Then someone must have taken him away and dumped him in the quarry. To hide the connection with the BRC.'

Simon frowned. It sounded wild and improbable, but . . . he ran his fingers over the creeper and thought about that figure on the wall.

'It did look like Lloyd.'

Dinah nodded miserably. 'I ought to have recognized him. But I got dazzled by—'

Her face changed completely. She caught her breath and grabbed at Simon's arm.

'I got dazzled by his torch!'

'So?' Simon couldn't see what she was getting at.

'So he didn't have the torch when we found him! He must have dropped it when he fell down.'

'So? What's that got to do with anything?'

'Don't you see? If we find the torch, that proves he was up at the BRC. People will have to listen to us then.' Dinah took a deep breath. 'I've got to go and look.'

'But that means going into the garden.'

'Of course. That's where the torch must be.'

Simon swallowed. 'If you're right, and they went to all that trouble to move Lloyd, that means they've got something to hide. It could be . . . dangerous.'

'That's why I've got to go,' Dinah said stubbornly. 'There's a mystery, and it's linked to Lloyd's accident. I'm going to go and find that torch.' She opened the door.

'Hang on,' Simon said. 'I'll come too. Do you want to go straight away?'

'There might not be any time to waste.'

Dinah's voice was calm, but Simon could hear that she was absolutely serious.

The woods behind the BRC were deserted. They climbed over the wall by the broken tree and dropped into the rhododendron bushes on the other side.

'Plenty of creeper here,' Simon said softly.

There was. It was draped all·over the bushes in long, tangled strands.

'But it's all *dead*.' Dinah picked up one of the shoots. There were little brown seed pods all over it, and they were ripe and dry. 'When we saw this last night, it was *growing*. Remember? It was above the top of the wall, higher than Lloyd's head. Things don't wither that fast.'

'This does. Remember my camera? The shoots that broke that were all withered by the time I got there.'

'But how?'

'Very fast growth.' Simon looked thoughtful. 'That's the kind of thing they work on here. Growing plants faster.'

'Plants?' Dinah frowned. 'I thought Dad said they had lizards.'

That didn't make sense to Simon. 'No, it's always been plants. My mother—' He stopped.

'Is that what she did?'

Simon nodded. 'She was working on a new sort of fast-growing rice, for places where ordinary rice won't grow. She went abroad to test it, and she got malaria.' He looked down at the creeper in Dinah's hand.

'I'm sorry,' Dinah said awkwardly.

Simon touched the creeper with one finger. 'Dad nearly went mad. He spent years going on about how the BRC had killed her. But now the new Director's arrived—he adores it.'

'What about your mother? Did she hate the place?'

Simon shook his head. 'She said she was doing work that would save people from starving to death. But that was before—'

'Before the new Director came,' Dinah said.

There was something odd about her voice. Simon looked up sharply, but she didn't explain. Whatever she thought, she was keeping it to herself.

'Let's look for that torch,' she said. 'We don't want to hang around here.'

She pulled a couple of seed pods off the withered creeper and looked at them for a moment. Then she pushed them into her pocket and glanced round.

'What's that funny little hill over there?'

Simon looked at it. Vaguely he remembered one of his father's stories. From the days when his father used to tell stories. 'I think it's an old ice house. Dad and his friends used to play there when they were little. Before the BRC came. There are tunnels underground, Dad said. Connecting it to the main house.'

'You mean . . . people could sneak up on us?' Dinah looked up at the BRC building and shuddered. 'Let's hurry and get out of here.'

Turning away from the ice house, she began to poke around in the bushes near the wall. Simon turned the other way—and saw a dead tree.

It had been dead for a long time. All the bark was gone, and the wood was rotten and crumbling. But that wasn't the strange thing about it. He ran his hand down the trunk.

'Dinah! Look at this tree.'

'What's the matter with it?' Dinah turned round.

'Something's been eating it. Scraping the wood away.'

'So? Lots of things eat rotten wood, don't they?'

'Not this much. *Look.*'

Dinah came across and looked, and her eyebrows went up. The tree had been a big one, but half of it was scraped away in regular, deep grooves. 'What on earth did that?'

'It's like—' Simon began. Then he shook his head. *It's like what wasps do*, he'd been going to say. But that was silly. It would take several million wasps to scrape away half a tree. Keeping his thoughts to himself, he reached out and broke off one of the scraped branches.

He was still staring at it when Dinah grabbed his arm and pointed.

'Look!'

Simon looked towards the house and his heart gave a single, huge thump. Six men in white lab coats were creeping down the garden. Not coming from the ice house, but sneaking across the lawn towards them.

When they saw that they had been spotted, the men stopped creeping and began to run.

'Wait!' one of them yelled. 'We want to talk to you!'

'Don't let them get us!' Simon hissed. 'Sprint!'

They headed for the wall at top speed. The moment Simon reached it, he jumped up, scrabbling for the top. But Dinah hesitated.

'Don't stop!' Simon yelled.

'But I've just seen Lloyd's torch! Under that bush!'

Simon flung one leg over the wall and looked down. He could see the torch, quite clearly, but it was too far away. The men were almost at the wall.

'There's no time to get it!' he panted. 'They'll catch you. Jump up here!'

Dinah scrambled up beside him and flung herself over the wall. Before the men were near enough to grab them, she and Simon were down in the wood, running as hard as they could. They didn't stop running until they reached the road.

'What would they have done?' Dinah panted. 'If they'd caught us?'

Simon shook his head. 'Don't know. But they weren't just scaring us off, were they? They were trying to get hold of us.'

'But *why*? Why is the BRC guarded so strictly?'

'It's the new Director. He hates people poking around. He—' Simon stopped, hunting for a way to explain. 'He's like a dark shadow on the village. Ever since he came, everything about the Research Centre has been deathly secret.'

'Because of the creeper?'

'Could be. Maybe it attacks people. That could be what happened to Lloyd.' Simon tried to imagine it. 'Maybe it grows so fast that it buzzes.'

'That's just guessing.' Dinah frowned. 'Guesses aren't any use to Lloyd. We've got to *find out*.'

Simon shook his head. 'It's hopeless. We haven't got anything to go on. We didn't manage to get the torch. We can't even identify the creeper.'

'The creeper! That's it!' Dinah stopped dead and grabbed his arm. 'What an idiot I am!'

'What are you talking about?'

'We can't identify the creeper—but an expert could.' Dinah pulled the dead strand out of her pocket and shook it under Simon's nose. 'Experts can identify plants by their DNA! We've got some real evidence after all!'

Chapter 7

'Just a Little Smear . . .'

They ran the rest of the way to the Hunters' house. Dinah knew just where to send the creeper. They had to post it off straight away. To an expert, who would see how peculiar it was. Then people would start investigating the BRC.

And they would discover what had happened to Lloyd.

She opened the kitchen door and led Simon in. As they went down the hall, they heard Mrs Hunter in the sitting-room. She was talking on the telephone and she sounded anxious and annoyed.

'Can't you get hold of him at *all?* This is the fourth time I've tried . . . Well, I'd better leave a message then. Yes, for Mr Bill Hunter. Please can you tell him that his son Lloyd has had an accident . . .'

'We'll go upstairs,' Dinah whispered.

DNA and Evolution was on the bookshelf by her bed. She snatched it up and flicked through the pages, looking for the sentences she remembered. When she found them, she pushed the book at Simon.

'Read this. And that bit there.'

Simon read out loud. '*Each living thing has its own, unique DNA, which took millions of years to evolve . . . It is now possible to identify a plant or an animal with complete certainty from tiny fragments of leaf or skin.*'

'You see?' Dinah said eagerly. 'We can send the creeper to this Professor Rowe, at the University of Wessex, and ask her to check its DNA. To see if it's really peculiar.'

'You think she would?'

'We can try. What have we got to lose?'

'Let's do it now,' Simon said. 'I'll write the letter while you're wrapping the creeper up.'

He wrote Dinah's address at the top of the paper and began the letter, while she wrapped up a handful of leaves from the creeper. By the time she had found an envelope, the letter was finished.

Dear Professor Rowe,

We read in your book, *DNA and Evolution*, that you can identify plants from their DNA. We are sending you a plant that Dinah's brother was holding when he was found unconscious. It is a very peculiar creeper that grows at unbelievable speed. Dozens of metres in a single night. Can you tell us what it is?

It's very important. Please help us if you can. There's no time to waste.

Yours sincerely,
Simon James and

'That's great,' Dinah said. She wrote her name after Simon's and wrapped the letter round the creeper. Then she pushed the whole lot into the padded envelope and stuck the flap down. 'I'll write *urgent* on the envelope.'

As she finished the address, there was a ring at the doorbell. A moment later, Mrs Hunter called up the stairs.

'Harvey! Dinah! Are you up there? We need you.'

'Drat!' Dinah held the parcel out to Simon. 'Can you post this? It sounds as though I might be busy.'

Simon tucked the parcel into his jacket. 'No problem.'

Mrs Hunter was in the sitting-room, talking to a small, round woman with untidy hair. As Dinah and Simon came downstairs, the woman smiled up at them.

'Hallo, Simon.'

He gave her a half smile in reply. 'Hallo, Doctor Gill.'

Doctor Gill? For a moment, Dinah couldn't think why the name was familiar. Then she remembered. This must be the doctor that Harvey had met at the bus stop. Another one who thought the BRC was wonderful.

'I suppose you're Dinah,' Doctor Gill said cheerfully. 'Well, I won't keep you long. Just going to do a little test on you all.'

'Test?' Harvey's voice said nervously. He was coming down the stairs behind Dinah and Simon. 'You mean . . . an injection or something?'

'Goodness me no!' Doctor Gill laughed briskly. 'Just a little smear from inside your cheek. That's all they want. It won't hurt a bit.'

'The hospital asked her to come,' Mrs Hunter said. 'They think Lloyd may have a virus. So they want samples from the three of us, to see if we've got it too.'

'Samples from inside our cheeks?' Dinah frowned. It all sounded a bit peculiar to her. She looked across the hall at Doctor Gill. 'You're not going to take blood samples?'

Doctor Gill's eyes slid sideways, avoiding Dinah's. She laughed again. 'No need for that. Just a little smear from inside your cheek. That's all they want.'

The same words, again. Simon caught his breath, and Dinah knew that he'd noticed too.

She swallowed. Then, casually, she said, 'Doesn't it take a blood test to show if we're carrying a virus?'

For a third time, Doctor Gill laughed. 'Goodness me no! Just a little smear from inside your cheek. That's all they want.' She seemed happy to go on saying it all day, but Mrs Hunter was in more of a hurry.

'Don't be tiresome, Dinah dear. The sooner we get these tests done, the sooner they can find out about Lloyd.'

Dinah bit her lip. 'Yes, of course. Sorry. Where shall we go?'

'In here will do fine.' Doctor Gill waved them into the sitting-room. 'I'm just going to brush the inside of your cheek with one of these.' She opened her bag and took out three small objects, like tiny toothbrushes.

Harvey frowned. 'What do you do with those?'

'I just brush your cheek inside—quite gently. Then I drop the brush into a bottle of liquid. Look.' She pulled out the bottles to show him. 'Then I whisk the bottles off to the hospital, at top speed. They'll see if the samples tell them anything that can help Lloyd.'

'Oh, I hope they do,' murmured Mrs Hunter. 'It's terrible not knowing what's wrong.'

Doctor Gill unwrapped one tiny brush. 'Who's going to be first?'

'You don't need me,' Simon said quickly. 'I'm off to the post office. Bye, Dinah.'

'Bye,' said Dinah.

She knew she sounded rather vague, but she was trying to remember where she had heard of cheek smears before.

What were they used for? Not testing for viruses, she was certain.

But *what?*

Simon knew. The moment Doctor Gill said *cheek smears,* he'd thought, *That's what the police use for DNA testing.*

And then he'd gone cold.

He and Dinah had just made up a parcel, to send something for DNA testing—and there was Doctor Gill, doing a DNA test on the Hunters. It was weird. Too much of a coincidence.

Like lots of things in the village these days.

Simon didn't know what was going on, but he had a feeling someone ought to keep an eye on Doctor Gill. To see what she did with those samples. As fast as he could, he ran round the corner, to his own house, to fetch his bike.

When Doctor Gill came out of the Hunters' house, he was hidden behind the post-box, ready to go. He waited until she was in her car, heading for the crossroads at the end of the village. Then he went after her, pedalling hard.

Doctor Gill was travelling fast too, as if the samples were urgent. Simon just managed to keep her in sight. He didn't mean to go far. All he wanted was to see her turn right, towards the hospital. Then he could go and post the parcel.

But she didn't turn right. She turned left, towards the BRC.

For a second, Simon just stared. Then he stood on his pedals and raced after her. As he turned left himself, he saw Doctor Gill pulling up outside the main entrance of the BRC. He pulled his bike into the shelter of the hedge and watched her get out of the car.

She opened her bag and took something out of it. Simon
had one glimpse of a small bottle before she walked up to the
guard at the gate. Her voice carried clearly down the road.

'Doctor Gill, to see the Director. Please will you let him
know I'm here.'

The guard glanced down at a clipboard and took out his
mobile phone. Doctor Gill went on standing there, with the
little bottle in her hand.

Simon could see exactly what it was. There was no
mistaking that bright blue cap. It was one of the sample
bottles she'd had at the Hunters' house. Inside it was one of
their DNA samples.

But whose?

And why would the Director of the BRC want it?

Someone appeared to take Doctor Gill into the building, and Simon cycled thoughtfully back, towards the Hunters' house. He wanted to tell Dinah what he'd seen. It was frightening to think about, but she ought to know.

He meant to tell her straight away, but as he came down the road, he saw something he wasn't expecting. He wasn't the only person heading for the Hunters' house. Three strange children were ahead of him, just turning in at the gate. There were two girls and a boy, all with rucksacks on their backs, and they were trailing up the path as if they were at the end of a long journey.

Simon hesitated. He was desperate to talk to Dinah, but maybe it wasn't the right moment. Not with strangers around. He waited at the corner, to see what happened.

The three children walked up to the front door and rang the bell. The moment the door opened, they all chorused cheerfully.

'Hallo, Di! Hi, Harvey!'

They were old friends. That was obvious, from the expression on Dinah's face. She ushered them in and shut the door, and Simon turned away, towards the post office.

As he reached the corner a car slid past him, driving up to the crossroads. A long, dark car, with a chauffeur and smoked glass windows. Simon couldn't see the passenger in the back, but he knew who it was.

The Director. Hurrying back to the BRC to meet Doctor Gill.

Simon shuddered and climbed back on to his bike. He had to get that parcel in the post. Straight away.

Chapter 8

The Fly

Inside the Hunters' house, there was a SPLAT reunion going on.

'But where's Lloyd?' Mandy said. She pulled off her rucksack. 'What have you done with him?'

There was a dreadful silence.

Ingrid looked sharply at Harvey and Dinah. 'There's something wrong, isn't there? That's why you didn't meet us at the station. You'd forgotten we were coming.'

Dinah went pink. 'I'm terribly sorry—'

'Never mind about that!' Ian said impatiently. *'What's wrong with Lloyd?'*

It was Mrs Hunter who answered. She came down the stairs with the car keys in her hand. 'It's going to take rather a lot of explaining. We'd better tell you on the way to the hospital.'

It didn't take long, because there wasn't much to say. Dinah didn't even try to explain about the BRC. She let her mother do the talking.

But even though they had been warned, Mandy and Ian and Ingrid were stunned when they looked through the glass into Lloyd's room and saw him lying surrounded by wires and tubes and machines.

'Doesn't he ever *move?*' Ingrid whispered.

'He will soon,' Mrs Hunter said quickly. 'I know he will.' She pushed the door open and looked back apologetically. 'I'm afraid you three can't come in.'

'Don't worry about us,' Mandy said. 'We'll go and find a drink or something.'

She went off down the corridor with Ingrid and Ian. Dinah and Harvey followed their mother into the room.

The light in there was harsh and bright, and every movement seemed exaggerated. The little blips on the monitor screen. The faint rise and fall of Lloyd's chest. Even the fly walking up the window pane. There was a nurse sitting beside Lloyd, and a doctor standing at the end of the bed, studying the charts.

'Is he . . . getting better?' Mrs Hunter murmured nervously.

The doctor's face told them that he wasn't.

Mrs Hunter tried again. 'What about those tests we had done?'

The doctor looked blank for a second and then shrugged. 'None of the tests shows anything.'

Mrs Hunter sighed and sat down beside the bed, staring at Lloyd's face as the doctor left. The monitors blipped on and on. Lloyd's chest rose and fell. The fly moved towards the top of the window pane. Dinah felt like crying. It looked as though things would never change.

And then something did change. A silly little thing, that she wouldn't normally have noticed at all. The fly reached the top of the window and began to buzz against the glass, looking for a way out. Bzzzzzz—

And Lloyd clenched his fists.

His eyes were still closed, but there was no mistaking it. He'd moved.

'Doctor!' the nurse beside the bed shouted.

The doctor came running back in. 'What's happened?'

'A reaction!' the nurse said, excitedly. 'Look at his fists.'

The doctor picked up Lloyd's wrist and felt the pulse. 'Did anyone speak? Or touch him?'

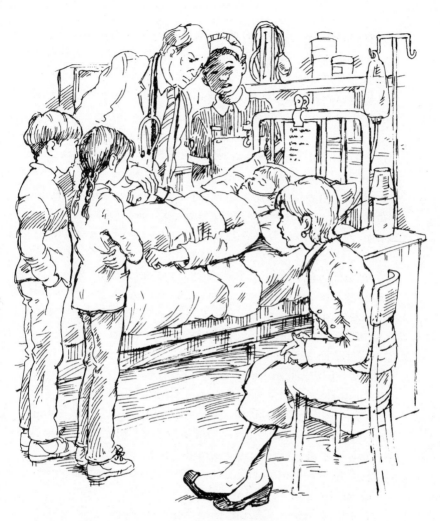

The nurse shook her head. 'No one did anything.'

'There was the fly . . .' Dinah said faintly.

The doctor gave her an impatient look. 'I'm talking about something significant.' He glanced over his shoulder. 'There shouldn't be a fly in here, anyway. Get rid of it please, nurse.'

The nurse opened the window, and the fly flew out. With a nod, the doctor turned back to the bed. Then he frowned.

'That's funny.'

Lloyd had relaxed again and his hands were hanging limp.

'It was the fly!' Dinah said fiercely. 'I know it was!'

She and Harvey were sitting in the kitchen with the rest of SPLAT, eating beans on toast, and crisps. The two of them were trying to explain a bit more about what had happened to Lloyd, but it wasn't easy. Whenever Dinah said anything, Harvey contradicted her.

She had been telling the others about the creeper, and seeing Lloyd on the wall, and the strange, chewed wood that she and Simon had found. But every time she said anything about the BRC, it made Harvey furious.

'Why do you keep going on about that? It's got nothing to do with Lloyd. He was in the quarry.'

Dinah sighed. 'I know we *found* him there, but—'

'But, nothing! You're obsessed with the BRC. That's why Lloyd had to follow you in the first place. And now you've got this bee in your bonnet about a fly!'

Ingrid giggled. 'A bee about a fly? That's very insecty.'

'It's all very insecty,' Ian said thoughtfully.

Mandy frowned. 'What do you mean?'

'Think about it,' Ian said. 'Dinah heard buzzing, didn't she? And she and Simon found some chewed wood. Well, wasps chew wood. To make their nests.'

'It hasn't got anything to do with wasps,' Harvey said crossly. 'Lloyd got stung by two wasps last year, and he was fine.'

Ingrid's eyes widened dramatically. 'But maybe it's a *giant* wasp! Maybe it ate that creeper of Dinah's and grew enormous.' Her eyes got even bigger. 'Maybe it *evolved*!'

The others groaned and threw crisp packets at her.

Dinah wished things were that simple. 'Nothing evolves that fast. It takes millions and millions of years.'

'What takes millions of years?' said a voice from the doorway.

They looked round and saw Rose standing there. None of them had heard her open the back door, but suddenly she was there in the kitchen, giving them all a sugary, sympathetic smile.

Ian, Mandy, and Ingrid all stared at her.

'*Rose?*' Ian said.

Mandy gulped. 'Where have you sprung from?'

'Wherever it was, you can go straight back there.' Ingrid sniffed loudly. 'We don't want people like you around.'

Rose didn't take any notice. She shut the door behind her and sat down on the bench next to Ingrid. 'I came to see how Lloyd was.'

Ingrid pulled a face and wriggled away, as far as she could without falling off the bench. 'What's Lloyd got to do with you?'

'I was the one who found him,' Rose said.

'That's right.' Harvey nodded. 'Don't be horrible to her, Ing. She's our friend, isn't she, Di? She's different now the Headmaster's gone.'

Rose shuddered. 'The Headmaster was a horrible man! Don't talk about him!'

She always uses the same words. Dinah glanced at Harvey, to see whether he'd noticed too, but he was grinning at Rose. And the others were grinning too. Rather cautiously, but as if they meant it.

'So . . . how *is* Lloyd?' Rose said.

'He moved a bit today,' said Harvey eagerly. 'The doctor thinks he reacted to something.'

Ingrid nodded. 'Dinah said it was the fly on the window, but the doctor wouldn't listen.'

Rose gave Dinah a sickly smile. 'You must find it really frustrating, not knowing what's wrong. No wonder you're thinking up silly explanations. You like finding things out, don't you?'

'Sometimes,' Dinah said stiffly.

Rose smiled again. 'But there's not much you can do about this. The doctors know best, don't they?'

No, they don't, Dinah wanted to say. But she wasn't going to start arguing with Rose. She stood up. 'I'm going to my room.'

The others looked surprised, but no one tried to stop her. As she walked across the hall, she heard Rose's voice, smooth and sly.

'I hope I didn't upset her. She's rather touchy, isn't she?'

'Dinah? Touchy?'

That was Mandy, sounding amazed. *Thanks, Mand,* Dinah thought. But it didn't help much. As she climbed the stairs, she felt very isolated.

If only someone would listen!

It was no use moping though. She looked severely at her reflection in the bedroom mirror. *Stop feeling sorry for yourself, Dinah Hunter! Blow your nose and cheer up!* She put a hand into her pocket, hunting for her handkerchief.

And her fingers closed round a hard, dry shape.

For a moment, she couldn't think what it was. Then she remembered and pulled it out, cradling it in the palm of her hand. It was one of the small brown seed pods she'd picked up in the BRC garden. The seeds from the creeper.

All ready to grow.

Suppose she planted them? She hadn't thought of it before, but suddenly it seemed a sensible idea. If she could grow some of the plants, she would have a chance to study them.

Slipping the seed pod back into her pocket, she crept downstairs. The others were still in the kitchen, and she could hear them talking excitedly.

'We ought to go up to the quarry and look for clues!' Ian was saying.

'Lloyd must have left a footprint or something!' (That was Ingrid.)

'It's better than sitting around being useless.' (That was Mandy.)

And then Rose's voice. 'You could look up at the top of the quarry. If he fell over the edge, he must have started up there.'

Dinah left them to get on with it. She wasn't sure of much, but she knew that the quarry was a red herring. All the real answers were at the BRC.

Letting herself out through the french windows, she went into the garden shed and found a seed tray. When she had filled it with earth, she took the seed pod out of her pocket.

Very carefully, she popped it open. Nine shiny brown seeds fell out into the palm of her hand. Using her little finger, she made nine holes in the damp soil and dropped the seeds in, one by one.

She was so busy that she didn't notice the sharp eyes watching her, through the kitchen window.

'Oh dear,' Rose was murmuring. 'Look at that.'

She pointed through the kitchen window and the others turned round and saw Dinah crouching in the back garden, grubbing around in the earth.

'I didn't know she was keen on gardening,' Rose purred.

Ingrid scowled. 'I don't know what she's doing, but I'm sure she's got a good reason.'

'That's right,' Mandy said loyally. She hesitated. 'All the same . . .'

Ian sighed. 'I know what you mean. It's a bit weird, isn't it? When Lloyd's so ill.'

'Oh, I'm sure she *does* care about Lloyd,' Rose said. 'Deep down.'

'Of course she cares!' Ingrid's scowl got fiercer. 'She'll be finished in a moment, and then we'll all go up to the quarry, to look for clues. That's what we do, isn't it, Harvey? We all stick together.'

'That's right,' Harvey said.

But he didn't sound quite as certain as Ingrid. After all, Dinah was being very peculiar.

Chapter 9

The Creeper Again

Dinah took the seed tray upstairs and put it on her window-sill.

'What are you doing?' said a voice from behind her.

'Mum!' Dinah spun round. 'You made me jump. I've just . . . planted some seeds.'

'That's nice,' Mrs Hunter said. 'I'm glad you're all so good at amusing yourselves. At least I don't have to feel guilty about neglecting you.'

She looked grey and tired. Dinah ran across the room and hugged her.

'Of course you don't have to feel guilty. We're fine. And we'll help as much as we can. Don't you think Dad ought to come back too?'

Mrs Hunter frowned. 'I haven't managed to speak to him yet. I've phoned the course centre and left a message, but they didn't seem to know where he was. I'll try again in a minute.' She sat down suddenly on the bed. 'Dinah, I want you to promise me something.'

'Of course,' Dinah said. 'Anything.'

'Promise me you won't sneak out at night again.'

Dinah went pink. 'I'm really, really sorry—'

'No, I'm not trying to make you feel bad. But I've got enough worry about Lloyd, without wondering whether the rest of you are creeping around in the dark. Promise me, Dinah.'

'I promise,' Dinah said.

'You're a good girl.' Mrs Hunter patted her hand. 'I'll go and have another try at phoning Dad then, while you get on with sowing your seeds.' She went out, shutting the door behind her, and Dinah turned back to the window-sill.

For a moment, she could hardly believe her eyes.

The seeds in the tray—the seeds that she had just pushed into the soil, a few minutes ago—were already sprouting. Tiny green leaves were poking through the earth.

She leapt out of her bedroom and ran downstairs to the kitchen. 'Quick!' she shouted as she pushed the door open. 'Come and see the seeds I've planted!'

She hadn't thought how it would seem to the others. They all stared at her, and Harvey went red in the face.

'You're *gardening*? When Lloyd's lying in hospital.'

Behind him, Rose gave a small, satisfied smirk. 'Don't be too hard on her, Harvey. Remember, it's different for you. Lloyd's your brother.'

Dinah glared at her. 'He's my brother too!'

'Only *adopted*,' purred Rose.

'It's exactly the same!' Dinah said, hotly. 'I care about him as much as Harvey does.'

Rose didn't say a word. She just looked down, slowly and elaborately. At the earth on Dinah's hands.

'You don't understand,' Dinah said stubbornly. 'This is important. The seeds—'

But Harvey was angry, and he wouldn't listen. He stood up and interrupted. 'We haven't got time to look at seeds now. We're just waiting to phone the hospital, after the doctors have been round. Then we're going up to the quarry, to look for clues.'

Mandy was watching Dinah's face. 'Are you coming?'

'Perhaps she's been there already,' Rose murmured. 'Looking for something that will help Lloyd. Maybe she's been there in secret, with Simon.'

'No I haven't!' Dinah snapped. 'I've *never* been to the quarry. Except when we went to get Lloyd. That's the only time I've been near the place.'

'But you're coming with us?' Ingrid said quickly.

'Yes. Yes, of course.' Dinah didn't think it would be any use, but they were SPLAT and they had to stick together. 'And while we're waiting—'

She suddenly realized that she needn't persuade them to go upstairs. She could bring the seeds down for them to see. Spinning round, she raced back up to her room.

The moment she opened the door, she could see that the creepers had grown. Their tiny seed leaves were already unfurling. For a moment, she was almost scared to think about it. Then she walked over to the window-sill.

She was just reaching out for the seed tray when there was a sound behind her. Spinning round, she saw Rose, standing beside the table in the corner. The table Dinah used as a desk.

Quick as a flash, Rose whisked her hands behind her back.

'What are you doing?' Dinah said suspiciously.

'I thought I'd come and look at these seeds of yours,' Rose purred.

Dinah had no intention of showing the seeds to her. She stepped sideways, blocking Rose's view of the window-sill. 'I haven't got time to show you now. We're going to the quarry.'

'Trying to keep in with the others, are you?' Rose said scornfully.

'I'm not *trying to keep in with them*. They're my friends.'

'Funny you're friends with such ordinary people,' Rose murmured. 'Don't you want friends who are more like you? Really *clever*.'

'They're not ordinary!' Dinah said angrily. 'And cleverness hasn't got anything to do with it. Clever people can be horrible. Look at the Headmaster!'

Rose's smug expression vanished. Her mouth twisted and she shuddered.

'The Headmaster was a horrible man! Don't talk about him!'

Those words again! Suddenly, in a chilling flash—Dinah understood. Every time anyone said *Headmaster*, Rose repeated the same message. It was meant to prove that she hated him, but it didn't really prove that at all.

It proved she was hypnotized. And that meant—

'He's back, isn't he?' Dinah said, before she could stop herself. 'The Headmaster's back!'

Rose shuddered again. 'The Headmaster was—'

'He's at the BRC, isn't he? The Headmaster is—'

'The Headmaster—' Rose began again.

'That's right!' Dinah said, triumphantly. 'The Headmaster, the Headmaster, the Headmaster!'

Rose's mouth scrabbled, opening and shutting helplessly, as though she couldn't cope with having the trigger word repeated over and over again. She looked like a machine that had suddenly broken down.

She's overloaded! Dinah thought. *It's too much for her!* She said it again, as fast as she could. 'The Headmaster, the Headmaster, the Headmaster!'

That was the last straw. Rose's eyes glazed over and she went completely rigid, like a robot. *I've got her!* Dinah thought. *Now the others will believe me!*

But Rose didn't stay long enough for that. She stepped backwards, out of the room, and before Dinah could move, she was running down the stairs and out of the front door.

Where was she going? Dinah flung herself downstairs, but she didn't go to the front door. Instead, she raced into the kitchen.

The others all looked round at her.

'What on earth—?' Harvey began.

'I can't come to the quarry,' Dinah panted. 'I've got to—'

But the moment she said *I can't come*, his eyes went cold. There was no hope of talking him round quickly. If she tried, she would lose Rose.

'See you when I get back,' she said.

Ingrid's mouth fell open, and Mandy looked upset, but it was no use worrying about that. Explanations would have to come later. The important thing now was to follow Rose.

Dinah slid out of the back door and crept along the side of the house. When she peered round the corner, she saw Rose disappearing up the lane, towards the crossroads. She was glancing back at the Hunters' house to see whether anyone was coming after her.

Dinah waited until she was round the first corner and then hurried after her. Rose turned left at the crossroads, towards the BRC. Exactly as Dinah had expected.

But she didn't stop at the BRC entrance. She walked straight on, like a robot. Right past the security guards and along the blank brick wall at the side of the building.

There was nothing else up the road except the woods. Surely she wasn't going there? Dinah crouched in the hedge just before the main entrance and watched.

Half-way along the wall, Rose stopped. She looked up and down the road, to check that there was no one about. Dinah cowered deeper into the bushes, ignoring all the thorns.

Rose obviously didn't see her, because she took something out of her pocket. Something small and black. She pointed it at the wall in front of her.

And the wall opened to let her in.

'She went into the BRC!' Dinah said. She sat down abruptly on Simon's bed. 'She flipped completely, and she headed straight for the BRC. I saw her go in!'

'So?' Simon couldn't see why she was getting so worked up. 'Doesn't her mother work there?'

'You don't understand. She didn't go in at the main entrance. There's a secret door at the side, opposite the big oak tree. She went in that way. *And she opened it with a remote control!*'

'What!' Simon stared. 'Why would anyone give her that?'

'She must be important.'

'Oh, come *on*!'

'No. I mean it.' Dinah looked down at her hands. 'I think there's something dreadful going on at the BRC. My family's involved somehow, and Rose has been sent to spy on us.'

Simon wondered whether she'd gone mad. But she had listened to him when everyone thought *he* was crazy. It was time he listened to her. 'Why *your* family?'

'I don't know, but someone at the BRC wanted us here. Dad didn't apply for the job he's got. They phoned up and asked him to come—for a huge salary. They even lent us a house so we could move straight away.'

'But it doesn't make sense.' Simon frowned. 'Why would they even know you existed?'

Dinah twisted her hands in her lap. 'There's someone we know. He hypnotizes people. And takes them over, so that they do what he says, and speak the words he gives them.'

That sounded horribly familiar. 'What for?' Simon said slowly.

'He wants to take charge of the world.'

It sounded like a bad joke, but Dinah was absolutely serious. 'Go on,' Simon said.

'He's come very close to it already. You don't have to take my word. Ask the others. He used to be the Head-master at our school.'

'And you think he's here?'

'I think he's the new Director of the BRC,' Dinah said steadily. 'And if he is, he won't be concentrating on new varieties of rice.'

'What about . . . something like that creeper? Would he have developed that?'

Dinah thought about it. 'Maybe. If he had a reason. But I don't think he's sticking to plants.'

'What do you mean?'

'Remember that buzzing we heard? Just before we saw Lloyd on the wall?'

Simon nodded.

'Well, I think it was an insect. When we were at the hospital this morning, there was a fly buzzing on the window. And Lloyd clenched his fists. As if he was frightened.'

'Of a *fly*?'

'Not the fly. The buzzing. I think it reminded him of . . . of whatever made him unconscious.'

Simon looked round his room, at the ants running round in their little tunnels, and the beautiful, fragile wasps' nest. He loved insects. But—

'You think they've been doing genetic engineering on insects? And developed something dreadful?'

'I'm sure they have.' Dinah was very pale, and her eyes were wide. 'But no one's ever going to believe me.'

'They will if we catch it,' Simon said grimly.

'*Catch* it?'

'I could set up an insect trap.'

'Inside the BRC's garden?' Dinah frowned. 'But it's dangerous in there. Look what happened last time.'

'I can go at night. I'll put the trap on that dead tree that's been chewed. That should catch anything flying round outside.'

'But suppose it's not outside,' Dinah said. 'Suppose they keep it inside?'

Simon looked at her. The answer seemed obvious to him, but she obviously hadn't thought of it. He took a deep breath.

'You've got to get hold of that remote control of Rose's. Then we can get inside too. At night, when the place is empty.'

For a moment, Dinah's eyes lit up. Then her face fell, and she shook her head. 'I promised Mum I wouldn't go on any more midnight expeditions.'

Simon shrugged. 'No hassle. You get the remote control, and I'll do the detective work. How about that?'

'You mustn't get caught,' Dinah said softly. 'The Director won't let you interfere with his plans. And it's no use arguing with him. He's absolutely sure he's right.'

'That makes it even more important to stop him,' Simon said gently. 'He mustn't be allowed to mess around with DNA research. Let me see how much I can discover about this insect thing.'

'All right,' Dinah said, reluctantly. 'And I'll try and find out more about the creeper. I've planted some of the seeds and they're growing already. Can I borrow your red torch, to see how they react to it?'

Simon took it out of the drawer. 'We need all the evidence we can get. If the Director's the person you think he is, there's no knowing what he might do. He might even—'

Simon suddenly remembered Doctor Gill and stopped. 'What's the matter?' Dinah said.

Simon didn't want to upset her, but he knew he had to tell her. 'You know those tests Doctor Gill did? The cheek smears? She didn't take them to the hospital at all. She took them straight to the BRC. I saw her.'

Dinah went white. 'I thought it was a funny way to test for a virus.'

Simon nodded. 'I don't think the Director's sticking to plants and insects. Or even lizards. I think he's interested in human DNA.'

Dinah stood up. 'We've got to stop him! I'm going to get SPLAT to help. When they hear all this, they'll *have* to join in.'

Half a mile away, four of the members of SPLAT were standing on a cliff, looking down into the quarry. They were staring down at the things in Harvey's hands.

A green pencil, and a notebook with a cat on it.

'I don't understand.' Mandy sounded bewildered. 'I thought Dinah had never been up here.'

'That's what she said.' Harvey began to flick through the notebook. It was Dinah's all right. There was no mistaking her neat, careful writing.

Every living thing has its own DNA . . .

Changes take millions of years to evolve into something useful . . .

Now things can be identified from DNA . . .

'You came here to get Lloyd,' Ingrid said defiantly. 'Dinah must have dropped the notebook then.'

'Yeah!' Ian looked relieved. 'That's what happened.'

Harvey shook his head unhappily. 'We didn't come up

here then. We drove straight into the bottom part, where
Lloyd was lying. If Dinah was up here, it must have been
some other time.'

'Perhaps someone else had the notebook,' Mandy said
hopefully.

Harvey shook his head. 'Who else would want it?'

'Well, I'm going to ask her!' Ingrid said. 'The moment
she comes back. I bet she's got a sensible explanation.'

'And if she hasn't?' Ian murmured.

'Then it looks as though Rose is right.' Harvey sighed.
'And Dinah's up to something peculiar.'

Chapter 10

Into the BRC!

Dinah could hardly wait to get back home, to talk to SPLAT. The moment she walked into the house, she knew they were there. She could hear them talking in the sitting-room.

But Rose was there too. Dinah could see her coat hanging up in the hall and hear her voice. It sounded perfectly —horribly—normal, as if she'd never flipped and headed for the BRC.

But she *had*. And maybe this was the chance to get her remote control and find out what was going on.

Dinah crept down the hall and felt in one of the pockets of Rose's coat. Her heart was thudding. She had never taken anything that didn't belong to her, and it was almost a relief to find that the pocket was empty. She slid her hand into the other pocket, half-hoping that would be empty too.

But it wasn't. Her fingers curled round a small plastic shape, about as big as a matchbox. Pulling it out, she saw that it was the remote control. A little black thing with a single blue button and a tiny light. Quickly, she pushed it into the pocket of her jeans.

She was only just in time. A split second later, Harvey opened the sitting-room door and stuck his head out. Dinah stepped back, guiltily.

'Oh. It's you.'

'Of course it's me,' Harvey said stiffly. 'Come in here. We want to talk to you.' He didn't smile. He'd never looked so unhappy and unfriendly.

What was going on? Dinah pushed her hands into her pockets, clenching a fist round the remote control, and walked into the sitting-room. Rose was sitting in the big armchair facing the door. She smiled faintly. The other three turned to look at Dinah with a strange, questioning expression.

'*Now* we'll get everything cleared up,' Rose purred, before anyone else could speak. 'Dinah's sure to have a sensible explanation.'

'An explanation for what?' Dinah said nervously. Very aware of the stolen remote control in her pocket.

Mandy reached into her bag. She took out a green pencil and a notebook with a picture of a cat on it and laid them on the coffee table.

'Recognize these?'

'Of course I do,' Dinah said. 'They're mine. What about it?'

'They were in the quarry,' said Ian. 'At the top of the cliff.'

'In the *quarry*?' Dinah frowned. 'What were they doing there?' They should have been in her bedroom. On the table.

'No need to be afraid,' Rose crooned. 'You can tell us the truth.'

'What are you talking about?' Dinah was bewildered. 'Why should I be afraid?'

'Tell us what you were doing at the top of the quarry,' murmured Rose. 'When Lloyd fell down.'

Dinah went cold. For a moment, she couldn't speak. Then she said, 'I've never been up there. I told you. Simon and I went to the BRC that night.'

She turned to Harvey, but he looked away, avoiding her eyes, and Rose went on relentlessly.

'Why don't you admit it? Lloyd was following you, and he fell over the edge. Didn't he? You won't tell anyone, because you're afraid you'll be blamed.'

'No! It wasn't like that at all!'

Rose just looked down at the notebook on the table.

'Nobody blames you, Di,' Ingrid muttered. 'We know it was an accident! You weren't very sensible, but anyone can panic.'

Dinah couldn't believe what they were saying. 'You think I saw Lloyd fall? And left him there?'

'He was following you,' Harvey said miserably. 'Why would he have gone to the quarry if you didn't go there?'

'Someone took him,' Dinah said. 'And dumped him there.'

'Oh come *on*!' Harvey looked impatient.

'Yes they did! Why won't you listen—?'

'Of course we'll listen,' Rose said smoothly. 'Just tell us how your notebook landed up at the quarry.'

For a moment, Dinah didn't know what to say. Then she remembered Rose coming into her room. Standing by the table, with her hands behind her back. Rose had stolen the notebook! She'd gone to the BRC for instructions and then put it in the quarry.

'I didn't drop that notebook!' Dinah said fiercely. '*You* took it. And planted it at the quarry.'

'Really?' Rose raised one eyebrow. 'Why would I do that?'

'Because—' Dinah began. Her hand was tight round the remote control. She was on the brink of pulling it out of her pocket and waving it in Rose's face, as proof of what she was up to.

But, just in time, she realized that she couldn't do it. Not if Simon was going to sneak into the BRC that night. Rose had to think she'd lost the remote control.

Dinah found herself standing with her mouth open stupidly, saying nothing.

'Some people always look for other people to blame,' Rose said slyly. 'Because they can't admit they're wrong.'

'I'm not wrong!' Dinah said. 'You're a spy and a traitor, Rose Carter—and I can prove it! Listen, everyone!' She walked up to Rose, and looked her straight in the eye. 'I know what you're doing. You're working for *the Headmaster*.'

Stepping back, she waited for Rose's face to twist. Waited for her to come out with the same words she always used, every time anyone mentioned the Headmaster.

But Rose didn't say a word. Her face stayed expressionless.

Dinah tried once more. 'Headmaster!' she said loudly.

It was no use. Rose stood there quiet and motionless.

Suddenly, Dinah realized what had happened, and she almost groaned out loud. Rose had been to the BRC, hadn't she? In a strange, trance-like state. The Headmaster must have ordered her to repeat what had happened—and then made sure that it couldn't happen again.

There was a long, horrible silence. Then one by one, the others turned away from Dinah, until only Rose was still looking at her. Dinah felt her eyes fill with tears. Spinning round, she raced out of the room, banging the door behind her.

She nearly bumped into Mrs Hunter.

'Dinah, *dear*! Whatever is the matter?'

Dinah wanted to tell her. She wanted it more than anything else in the world. But that would mean explaining everything. Even the remote control. And if she did that, her mother would make her give it back, and Simon would never get into the BRC.

Dinah forced a smile on to her face. 'Nothing's the matter. I'm just on my way to Simon's house, and I've got to hurry. Or I won't be back before it's dark.'

'You're a good girl.' Mrs Hunter touched her hand. 'I know you'll keep your promise.'

Dinah almost ran out of the door. All the way to Simon's she was thinking, *Simon's GOT to find out what's going on at the BRC. I can't bear this much longer* . . .

When Dinah knocked on his door, Simon had just finished sorting out the things for the insect trap. He ran downstairs with a tin of treacle in one hand and some garden netting over his arm.

'Did you get it?' he said eagerly.

Dinah plunged a hand into her pocket and pulled out a little piece of black plastic. She pushed it at him, as if it were too hot to hold. 'There you are,' she said fiercely. 'You are going soon, aren't you?'

'I'll go now. I've got everything ready.' Simon looked at her. 'Are you all right?'

'I'm fine,' Dinah said stiffly. 'Is that for the trap?' She pointed at the treacle.

Simon nodded. 'It's to attract the insects. And the net's for catching them. I'll fix them up, and by that time the BRC should be almost empty. And then—' He waved the remote control and dropped it into his pocket. 'I'll come round tomorrow and tell you all about it.'

'You will . . . be careful, won't you?' Dinah said nervously.

'Simon the Super-Spy, that's me. Don't worry. I'll be round at nine tomorrow morning. Promise.'

Dinah lifted a hand to wave him goodbye. When he turned at the corner of the road, she was still watching, looking pale and tense. Simon waved again, reassuringly. Then he tucked the net into his jacket and set off for the woods.

It was very dark up there, but Simon didn't risk using a torch. He felt his way along the wall and climbed over quietly and carefully, wriggling through the bushes to the dead tree.

The treacle tin made an awkward lump in his pocket. He took it out and smeared the tree trunk lavishly with sticky black treacle. Then he hid the half-empty tin behind the tree trunk. He'd be better off without that while he was sneaking round the BRC.

Carefully, he draped his net over the dead branches. It hung round the sticky trunk like a tent, ready to entangle anything that was lured by the smell of the treacle. By the time it was in place, Simon's hands were covered in treacle too. He bent down to wipe them on the damp grass.

And he heard a familiar noise, coming from the direction of the old ice house.

Bzzz-ZZZ-zzz-ZZZ.

Whatever it was, it was stirring. He smiled grimly. He'd better get out of the way and let the treacle do its work.

Glancing up the garden, towards the main BRC building, he saw that it was dark already, except for a single light on the ground floor. The light that never seemed to go out.

That was the place he ought to head for.

Working his way back to the wall, he scrambled over and padded out to the road. There was no one in sight. He walked down as far as the big old oak tree, and looked at the wall that was facing him.

There was no sign of a door. For a moment, he wondered whether he was in the right place. But Dinah had sounded quite definite. *Opposite that big oak tree.* Taking out the remote control, he pointed it at the wall and pressed the blue button.

Slowly and silently, a section of wall swung inwards, leaving a dark open doorway.

Taking a deep breath, Simon stepped through. He pressed the remote control again, to close the door. Then he turned on his torch. Dinah still had the red one, so he'd had to bring an ordinary white torch, and it looked terrifyingly bright.

Straight in front of him was a steep flight of steps leading down to a tunnel. It curved away towards the woods, and Simon guessed that it was one of the tunnels that led to the ice house. But he hadn't got time to investigate that.

Instead, he took the corridor on the left that stayed at ground level, twisting into the main building. He crept along it, quietly and carefully, until he came to another flight of steps leading down to the tunnels.

At the top of the steps was a closed door with light showing all round the edges and through the keyhole. Kneeling down, Simon put his eye to the keyhole.

He found himself peering into a bright, modern laboratory, like the one where his mother had worked when he was little. He couldn't see all of it, but what he could see looked very familiar. Long benches. Computer terminals. Fridges for storage and shelves full of bottles. The only unexpected thing was the glass tank full of little green lizards, right next to the big computer screen.

There were half a dozen white-coated technicians working at the benches, but Simon didn't spot anyone he knew. The whole place looked boring and ordinary.

Suddenly, brisk footsteps sounded from the other end of the laboratory, and a man walked into view, from the part that was out of sight. He was tall and thin, with pale hair and a narrow, colourless face. Simon had never seen that face before, but he knew exactly who it was.

The Director.

There was something unmistakable about the way he stood. Looking round the room with a sharp, commanding expression. Simon found himself holding his breath. Wondering what the man's eyes were like, behind his dark glasses.

Then the Director spoke. His voice was very precise and clipped.

'State. Progress. Of. Experiment.'

From the computer in front of him came an answering voice.

'Experiment. Satisfactory.'

He glanced sideways, towards the area of the laboratory he had just left, and his lips curved in a small, triumphant smile. Simon angled his head uncomfortably sideways, trying to find out what he was smiling at. And, for the first time, he saw what was at the far end of the room.

An egg.

But not an ordinary egg. It was lying in a large glass tank with a panel of dials and gauges at one end. It was smooth and white and beautifully rounded.

And it was over a metre long.

That's impossible! Simon was so stunned that he didn't realize that he'd gasped out loud. Not until the Director raised his hand. And four of the technicians began to walk swiftly towards the door.

Chapter 11

Strange Things Growing

Simon . . .

That was Dinah's first thought as she opened her eyes. How had he got on? Had he found out anything?

Her room was still pitch dark and she reached for the alarm clock, to see how many hours she had to wait before he came round. How long was it until nine o'clock?

The alarm clock said five past nine.

What? It looked more like midnight. Dinah sat up sharply and switched on the bedside light, to look at her watch.

Five past nine.

Jumping out of bed, she ran to the window and pulled the curtains open. And then she saw why her room was so dark. The creepers in the seed tray had grown so much that they were blocking her window. Their long, thick shoots were pressed tightly against the glass, shutting out the daylight. They must have flowered in the night, but the pale flowers were already dropping. In their places, tiny seedpods were swelling.

These creepers were growing even faster than the one Simon had photographed.

Dinah snatched up the red torch she'd borrowed from Simon and switched it on. The effect was dramatic. Slowly but unmistakably, all the shoots twisted away from the glass and began snaking towards her. She waved the torch first left and then right, and the creeper followed it, twisting eerily.

She had never got dressed so fast. In a couple of minutes, she was racing down to the kitchen.

'Harvey! Mandy! Everyone! Come here.'

Harvey came out of the kitchen. 'Oh, there you are. We thought you were *never* getting up. Mum went off to the hospital an hour ago.'

'Come and see why I slept so long!' Dinah said. 'It was that creeper—'

Harvey started to pull a face, but she didn't let him say anything. She grabbed his sleeve.

'Look—you've got to listen. I don't usually fuss about nothing, do I?'

Ingrid appeared behind Harvey's shoulder. 'No, she doesn't. You know she doesn't, Harvey.'

'That's right. Let's see what this is all about.' Mandy was there as well now, with Ian close behind. 'Show us, Di.'

Dinah didn't see how they could bear to walk up the stairs so slowly. She raced ahead, turning back towards them as she flung open her bedroom door.

'Look!'

They looked.

There was a long silence.

'You brought us up here to see *that*?' Ian said at last.

All the creepers were completely dead. Their long, shrivelled shoots were hanging down over the radiator. Brown and withered.

'But . . . but I don't understand,' Dinah stuttered. 'They weren't like that just now. They were alive.'

'They *can't* have been,' Ingrid said. 'Look at them.' She marched across and lifted one of the shoots. It crumbled in her hand.

'They can't all be dead,' Dinah said desperately. She turned on Simon's torch and began waving it about.

Harvey stared. 'What are you doing?'

'Those shoots were following the torch. Just a few minutes ago. They were green and alive, and they were moving.'

Gently, Mandy took the torch away and switched it off. 'Well, they're not moving now.'

Dinah couldn't believe it. Even though she knew it was stupid, she tried to take the torch back, but Harvey grabbed it and jammed it into his pocket, so that she couldn't get it.

'You're obsessed,' he said bitterly. 'You don't care about Lloyd at all.'

'I do!' said Dinah. 'I do! That's why—'

But it was no use. They were all edging away from her. Well, let them! Lifting her chin resolutely, she marched past them, to the stairs. She was going to talk to Simon. *He* would understand that she had discovered something important.

As she reached the front door, the phone started to ring. She turned back to answer it, but at that moment the back door opened and Rose's voice called through it.

'Hallo! Is there anyone in?'

That was the last straw. Dinah wrenched the front door open. Someone else could answer the phone. *She* was going to Simon's!

'He's not here,' Mr James said, scowling at Dinah. 'Looks as though he stayed out all night.'

'All night?' Dinah's throat went dry. 'Do you know where he is?'

Mr James just scowled.

'I think I know.' Dinah bit her lip. 'He did say he was going to the BRC—'

Immediately—unbelievably—Mr James's surly face changed. He smiled broadly.

'The BRC is a wonderful thing to have in the village. It's a really good neighbour.'

Dinah felt like screaming. But she wouldn't let herself. *Use your brain, Dinah Hunter*, she thought sternly. *See what you can find out.*

'Did you always think it was wonderful?' she said quickly.

Mr James shrugged. 'I had my ideas in a bit of a muddle. Until the new Director came down to that meeting.'

'What's he like? The new Director.'

'Tall, thin fellow. In dark glasses.'

Dinah's heart thumped, but she forced herself to stay calm and ask the next question. 'Did he . . . take his glasses off at all?'

'Not sure. It's a funny thing, but I was rather sleepy that evening.' Mr James looked suspiciously at Dinah. 'Why?'

'Oh, nothing.' Dinah said it as lightly as she could, but her heart was sinking. 'Don't you think you ought to phone the police? About Simon.'

That was the end of Mr James's good temper. He glared at her. 'Don't you tell me what to do, madam. *I'll* decide when it's time to phone the police. And I'll give Simon a good belting when he does turn up.'

He shut the door in Dinah's face.

For a moment she stood there, with her brain whirling.

A tall, thin man . . . dark glasses . . . I was feeling rather sleepy . . .
It was the Headmaster all right. But what was he up to?

And what had he done with Simon?

'You can't just keep me prisoner!' Simon said defiantly. He wriggled against the straps that tied him to the chair.

'Can't?' said the Director. He was inspecting the remote control that the technicians had found in Simon's pocket. 'I see no problem.'

'What about all the people who work here?'

The Director didn't even bother to reply. He simply looked round. Everyone in the lab where they were had gone back to work, completely ignoring Simon.

'My father will phone the police!' Simon shouted.

'The police think the BRC is wonderful,' the Director said absently. He was hardly bothering to listen. 'And so does your father.' He nodded at one of the technicians and held out the remote control. 'Return this to Rose Carter. Discreetly. And tell her to be more careful where she leaves it.'

As the man slid out of the room, Simon made a last attempt to protest.

'My friend will come looking for me!'

That did get the Director's attention. Suddenly, and unexpectedly, he smiled. It was a cold, thin-lipped smile, more terrifying than any glare.

'Ah, yes. Your friend. Miss Dinah Hunter.'

Simon wished he hadn't mentioned Dinah, but it was too late now. The Director was walking towards the glass tank at the end of the room.

'Let's see if we're ready for Dinah Hunter,' he said softly.

For a moment, he stared down at the huge, pale egg inside the tank. Then he turned towards the computer and spoke.

'Report. On. Experiment.'

Words spread across the screen, and echoed from the speakers as the computer answered.

'Approximate. Time. To. Hatching. One. Hour.'

The Director smiled his thin-lipped smile again. 'Check. Temperature.'

'Current. Temperature. Ideal. For. Hatching.'

Simon couldn't bear it. Struggling against the straps again, he yelled at the Director's back. 'You leave Dinah alone! I don't know what's in that egg, but I bet it's something foul! Don't get Dinah involved!'

The Director turned and gave him a long, cool stare. 'That is very amusing,' he said at last.

'*Amusing?*'

'You would like to share the joke?' The Director turned and spoke to the computer. 'Display. DNA. Processing.'

The computer screen cleared, and refilled with a complex, spinning image. A double, twisted shape, with links running between the two sides, like a spiral ladder.

DNA of lizard, said the letters.

The Director waved a hand towards the small glass tank beside the computer. 'One of those lizards,' he murmured. 'An admirably unemotional creature.'

Simon looked at the tiny green lizards in the tank. 'What did you do to it?' he growled.

'The process is fully automated,' the Director said briskly. 'All I had to do was feed a lizard into the analysis chute.' He pointed to a large round hole that gaped just below the screen. 'The chute was designed to cope with any living organism. Except . . .' He gave a small, dry smile. 'Except perhaps an elephant.'

Simon shuddered. 'You mean . . . you killed it?'

The Director looked scornful. 'That is a ridiculously emotional word. The lizard's DNA has been recorded. I can reproduce that individual lizard whenever I choose. But, better than that, I can . . . improve on it.'

He turned back to the screen, just as it divided into two windows. In the first was the lizard's DNA, spinning as before. In the second another double helix appeared.

DNA of Dinah Hunter, said the letters underneath.

Simon swallowed. 'The cheek smear,' he said softly. His voice seemed to stick in his throat.

'Exactly.' The Director smiled. 'Why do you think I brought the Hunters here? I needed Dinah Hunter's DNA, because it includes genes for outstanding intelligence. Unfortunately, in Dinah herself, those genes are combined with others that produce wasteful emotions and feelings.'

Simon couldn't speak. He stared at the two spinning shapes, as if he were in a trance.

'Imagine how much better the human race would be,' the Director crooned, 'if it combined both sets of genes. Dinah's intelligence. The lizard's lack of emotion.' He turned back to the screen. 'Here is what we did with our DNA samples, in this laboratory.'

On the screen, the DNA spirals were unzipping, so that each one made two separate strands. Suddenly Simon realized what was going to happen, and he leaned forward so sharply that the straps cut into his arms.

'No!' he whispered in horror. '*No!*'

But he couldn't stop what was happening on the screen. The division between the two windows dissolved, and the broken strands of DNA floated together.

Chapter 12

Telephone Treachery

Dinah ran all the way home and flung open the kitchen door.

'Hallo,' said Rose.

She was sitting in a chair, staring at the door. Waiting.

Dinah scowled at her. 'I don't want to talk to you.'

'There's no one else to talk to,' Rose said smoothly. 'They've all gone out.'

'What do you mean? Where are they?'

'You would know that,' Rose purred, 'if you hadn't run off when the telephone rang. But I can see why you wanted to get away. The others aren't really your kind of people, are they? Too stupid.'

'You're the one who's stupid,' Dinah said. 'They're my friends. Where have they gone?'

Rose looked her straight in the eye. 'I don't know.'

It was a lie. Dinah knew it was a lie. She was wondering how to make Rose tell her the truth when the telephone rang again. Squeezing past Rose's chair, she walked into the sitting-room and picked up the receiver.

'Hallo,' she said. 'Is that you, Harvey?'

'No, it's me.'

'*Simon!* Where are you?'

'Hallo, Dinah,' Simon said. His voice sounded curiously flat. 'I'm in the BRC. You've got to come here. It's urgent.'

'What's going on?'

Simon didn't answer the question. Instead, he repeated what he'd said before. In exactly the same voice.

'I'm in the BRC. You've got to come here. It's urgent.'

A horrible chill crept slowly up Dinah's spine. 'Did you get caught?'

'I'm in the BRC. You've got to come here. It's urgent.'

Dinah knew just how he must be looking. Blank-faced. Obedient. And she knew who else was listening to the conversation. The person who had given him those words to say.

'You've got to come,' Simon said again.

Dinah closed her eyes. She wanted to rescue Simon, but she *couldn't* go to the BRC. Not if the Headmaster wanted her there. She would be walking straight into his hands, and that wouldn't help anyone.

'I'm sorry,' she said, as gently as she could. 'I can't come. But I know what's happened. And I'll get you out of there, as soon as I can.'

That didn't seem to make any impression on Simon. He began to repeat the same sentence again in exactly the same blank voice. 'I'm in the BRC—'

Dinah couldn't bear it. She took the receiver away from her ear and for a moment the words echoed in the air. *You've got to come here. It's urgent.* Then she rang off.

'Problems?' said Rose's voice from the doorway.

Dinah turned round and glared. 'It's nothing to do with you. Why don't you go home?' Then she had a better idea. 'No. Why don't you go back to the BRC? And *your friend* the Director.'

Rose's eyes flickered. 'I don't know what you're talking about.'

'It's no good trying to fool me. I know what's going on. But you're not going to get away with it.'

'No?' Rose said softly.

'No!'

Dinah pushed past her. She didn't know where she was going, but she knew that she had to get out of the house and *do* something. If she went on standing there, she would go mad.

But she had only reached the door, when the phone rang yet again. She dived back towards it, but Rose was there first.

'Yes?' she said, with her eyes on Dinah. Cold, calculating eyes.

'Give that to me,' Dinah said.

Rose ignored her, listening to the voice at the other end of the line. 'Yes, she's here,' she said, after a minute. 'Yes. You want her to come? It's urgent?'

That sounded like Simon again. Dinah felt sick. With a brittle smile, Rose held out the receiver, her hand over the mouthpiece.

'Simon wants to speak to you.'

Dinah wasn't sure she could bear it. Not that horrible, dead-sounding voice.

'Hurry up,' murmured Rose. 'He said, *I'm at the BRC. She's got to come here. It's urgent.*'

Dinah shook her head. 'I don't want to speak to him,' she said miserably.

Rose uncovered the receiver and spoke into it. 'Dinah won't come.'

The voice at the other end gabbled insistently. Dinah couldn't catch the words, but Rose held the receiver out again. 'He says you've got to. He says it's urgent.'

'I know what he says,' Dinah muttered bitterly.

She felt like crying. Snatching the receiver out of Rose's hand, she spoke into it quickly, while she could still keep her voice steady.

'Look—I mean it. I'm not coming. It would be a really silly thing to do. I'm going to collect some evidence instead.' She hunted for a word that might jolt Simon awake. A word that would mean nothing to the Head-master, if he was listening. There was only one she could think of. '*Treacle!*' she said fiercely.

Almost before she had finished saying it, the phone went dead.

'What?' Dinah looked down at the receiver. 'He's gone.'

Then she realized that there was no dialling tone. Sharply, she looked up. Rose was standing by the telephone point, with the plug in her hand.

'You cut me off!' Dinah said.

Rose smirked. 'You'd better go and *collect your evidence*, hadn't you? If it's so important.'

Grabbing the plug out of her hand, Dinah shoved it back into the socket, but it was too late. Whoever had been at the other end of the line had gone.

Ten miles away, in the hospital, Harvey stood looking at another telephone.

'She wouldn't come,' he said. Stunned.

'*What?*' Mandy stared at him.

'You can't have explained properly,' Ingrid said. 'She wouldn't refuse. Not if she knew how important it was.'

'She knows,' Harvey said miserably. 'Rose was there. I asked her if she'd told Dinah, and she said yes.'

'You mean . . . Dinah knows Lloyd's getting worse?' said Ian.

Harvey nodded.

'The doctor said we *all* had to talk to him!' Mandy was almost in tears. 'Dinah's voice might get through, even though ours didn't. It's his last chance!'

Harvey looked grim. 'Rose told her that too. But she still won't come.'

Ingrid shook her head. 'So what *did* she say?'

'Something about treacle,' muttered Harvey. 'And collecting evidence. And then she disconnected the phone.'

Ingrid shook her head. 'She's flipped, hasn't she? Really flipped. What are we going to do about her?'

'Who cares about Dinah?' Harvey said bitterly. 'It's Mum I'm worrying about. How am I going to tell her that Dinah won't come?'

Chapter 13

Hatching

'So,' murmured the Director. 'We need a different plan . . .'

Simon opened his eyes, suddenly aware of the straps cutting into his arms. Had he been asleep? He felt exhausted, as if he'd been struggling against a heavy weight.

'What's going on?' he muttered. 'Did I—?'

'You have just been speaking on the telephone,' the Director said crisply. 'Begging Dinah Hunter to come here.'

'I was asking Dinah to come here?' For a moment, Simon couldn't believe it. Then, with a shiver, he remembered what Dinah had said about the Director. 'You hypnotized me!'

An expression of distaste crossed the Director's face. 'It was an inefficient waste of energy. You are not a good subject. Almost as difficult as Lloyd and Harvey Hunter.'

'But I did what you wanted.' Simon found himself shaking. He felt horribly alone and afraid. 'Did I get Dinah to come? Into a trap?'

The Director smiled thinly. 'No, you failed. You begged her, but she refused. So much for friendship. So much for feelings. Don't you see how much better my creature will be, without them?' He turned towards the computer. 'Display. Best. Possible. Qualities. Of. Hunter. Lizard. DNA. Mix.'

The computer screen filled with lines of words and

figures. Simon leaned forward to read them and the numbers whirled in his head.

Physical strength	125
Intelligence level	250
Obedience	300
Speed of growth	350
Emotional sensitivity	004

Below the figures, a message flashed. *Develop this creature? Y/N*

'You can't develop it!' Simon said. 'It wouldn't have any feelings. It would be a monster.'

'You are too late,' the Director said calmly. 'What do you think is waiting to hatch out of that egg?'

He turned and pointed down the laboratory. As if he were in a nightmare, Simon felt his eyes travel helplessly towards the glass tank.

'Exactly!' The Director walked across to the tank and stood over it. 'As soon as I received Dinah Hunter's cheek smear sample, I mixed her DNA with the DNA of one of those lizards. Then I programmed the computer to consider all possible combinations of those genes. To select the one most suited to my purpose.'

'But that was only yesterday.' Simon stared at the egg. 'It can't have reached that stage already.'

'No?' The Director raised an eyebrow. 'You forget all the work these laboratories have done on speeding up growth.'

'That was meant to *help* people.'

An expression of distaste crossed the Director's face. 'You mean it was wasted. Until I came, this research centre concentrated on producing food for unnecessary people.

But I have used that research intelligently. To speed up my experiments.'

'But nothing's meant to grow that fast!' yelled Simon. 'It's unnatural!'

'Unnatural?' the Director said disdainfully. 'Nature has had its day. I have replaced natural selection with computer selection. Under my control.'

'That's monstrous!' Simon shouted. 'It's impossible!'

'It is efficient. And it is about to reach its climax. *Now!*' The Director looked at his watch and spun round to the big glass tank at the end of the lab.

There was a loud snapping noise from inside the tank. Simon's eyes swung back to the egg, and he saw a long, dark crack appear across the top of it. His mouth went dry.

'The summit of evolution,' the Director said softly. 'The creature that will take over the world.'

There was a scrabbling sound, and the crack widened. Slowly, an elbow emerged. Then a whole arm, straightening as it wriggled free of the shell.

Simon felt sick. The arm was pale and smooth-skinned and slightly freckled. As far as he could see, it looked uncannily like Dinah's arm.

Except that it ended in scaly green fingers, with sharp claws.

At that moment, Dinah herself was running towards the BRC. But she wasn't heading for the building. She was making for the woods at the back.

Treacle, she'd said on the phone. And that was what she was going to look at now. The insect trap was the only

thing left. The only place where she might find more evidence of what was going on.

It would have been safer to wait until dark, but things were moving too fast for that. She would just have to be careful. She climbed over the back wall of the BRC and wriggled her way along the ground inside, keeping under cover as she worked her way towards the dead tree and Simon's net.

She had no idea what to expect. Would the net be

empty? Would it be full of moths? Or would there be something monstrous and alien tangled in its meshes?

There certainly wasn't anything big there. She could see that, even from the far side of the clearing. But the net looked peculiar. Something had obviously happened to it.

Cautiously Dinah stood up and ran the short distance across the clearing, making sure that the tree's solid, gnawed trunk hid her from the house. As she got closer, she saw that the treacle on the tree trunk was marked with long scored lines. There had been something in the net, but it wasn't there any more.

It was only when she reached the tree and spread the net out in her hands that she realized what had happened. Whatever had been tangled up in it had gnawed its way out. The net was a strong one, but something had chewed through the mesh, to make a hole at least two metres long.

The severed ends were ragged and irregular. Dinah touched them and drew her hand away quickly, in disgust. They were coated with something glutinous and sticky.

Like spit.

Reaching up, she unhooked the net from the dead branches and bundled it up. It was disgusting, but it was the nearest thing she had to a clue. She saw Simon's treacle tin under the tree and picked that up too.

She was just pushing the treacle tin into her pocket when there was a noise further up the garden. From the direction of the ice house.

Bzzz-ZZZ-zzz-ZZZ.

Dinah's heart thudded. Dropping on to her hands and knees, she began to crawl towards the ice house, still keeping under cover.

From the back, the ice house was just a low, green mound. But when she crawled round to the front, she saw steps going down, below ground level. They led to a little door in the side of the mound.

Obviously it wasn't opened much. There was a tangle of the strange creeper in front of it and it looked well established. The live, green strands were twined round great bundles of withered dead ones.

Dinah stood up and crept down the steps, towards the door. Now she was so close, she could tell that the buzzing came from behind it. At every step, it sounded louder.

Bzzz-ZZZ-zzz-ZZZ.

With her free hand, she parted the strands of creeper, looking for the door handle. What she found instead was a black hole. The wood of the door was rotten, and it had been scraped away—like the wood of the dead tree. There was a large hole, just above Dinah's eye level.

The buzzing seemed very loud now. Holding her breath, Dinah stood on tiptoe, trying to see through the hole. But it was pitch dark inside the ice house.

She was just wondering whether to risk opening the door, when she heard a rustle of leaves behind her. And the sound of low voices, coming down the garden.

Desperately, she scuttled up the steps, away from the door. Making for the nearest patch of rhododendrons, she burrowed in, as deep as she could.

She was just in time. A few seconds later, two men in white coats walked into the clearing. They made straight for the ice house and hesitated at the top of the steps. Dinah thought they looked nervous. Almost frightened.

Finally, they walked down the steps to examine the

door. Like Dinah, they parted the shoots of creeper. The moment they saw the hole, they backed away up the steps again, and stood muttering to each other.

Dinah strained to hear what they were saying, but she only managed to catch a few words.

'. . . must be getting out that way . . . have to tell the Director . . .'

'. . . can't risk going in . . .'

They sounded terrified.

It seemed a long time before they moved, but at last they walked back up the garden. Dinah crawled out of the rhododendron bush, feeling shaken but triumphant. She had the net. And she knew where the buzzing was coming from. Some evidence at last.

She wriggled back to the wall, pushed the net inside her jacket and scrambled over. The moment she was safely down on the other side, she started running.

She had to get the others to come back to the BRC with her. If they were all there, they could break into the ice house and find out what was buzzing.

So that Lloyd could be cured, and Simon could be rescued from the Director.

Chapter 14

Ready for Testing

Simon had stopped struggling. He was staring across the laboratory, in horrified fascination, watching the figure at the computer terminal.

The lizard-girl.

She was gazing at the screen, and moving the mouse deftly. Not with the scaly claw that Simon had seen at first, but with her other hand. The one that looked like Dinah's.

The rest of her looked like Dinah too. That was obvious, in spite of the heavy headphones she was wearing, and the baggy track suit they'd dressed her in. She had the same thin face and dark hair. And she was watching the computer screen with the same intelligent, absorbed eyes. The only difference was that lizard hand and the patch of small green scales on her right cheek.

And the fact that she had no feelings. Simon shuddered.

'Enough!' the Director said suddenly. He reached down and pulled the headphones off the girl's head. 'Time to test how much speech you have learnt.' He bent down and spoke slowly. 'What is your name?'

The lizard-girl spun round in her chair. Her voice was rough and unpractised, but she didn't hesitate. 'I have no name,' she said stiffly.

'What name would you like?'

'Whatever you choose,' the girl said, without expression.

The Director smiled. 'That is the answer I expected. Very good. Your name is Eve.'

'Thank you, sir.'

'You have mastered the speech program very fast. Now we must move on to serious testing.'

'She's only just been born,' Simon muttered. 'What's the hurry?'

'You think she should waste time on *childhood*?' the Director said icily.

'Childhood's not a waste—'

'It is inefficient and unproductive. Eve was designed to grow fast, and she is already as mature as Dinah Hunter. It is time for them to meet.'

'To *meet*?'

'Of course. How else am I to test Eve? She was designed as a superior version of Dinah Hunter. To test her, I must pit the two of them against each other.'

Simon didn't like to think what the Director meant by *pit them against each other*. 'Dinah won't come!'

'I think she will.'

The Director picked up the telephone beside him and tapped at the buttons. As he did so, Simon glanced sideways, at Eve. He smiled, just to see what would happen.

Nothing happened. She stared straight through him. As if she were a lizard.

The phone rang for a moment and then Simon heard a voice answering from the other end. A smile spread across the Director's face.

'Mrs Hunter? Good afternoon. I am the Director of the Research Centre. I understand that your son Lloyd has had an accident.'

Mrs Hunter's voice gabbled at the other end of the line. Simon held his breath and listened hard, but he couldn't make out the words. What was going on?

'*Most* unfortunate,' said the Director, when the voice stopped. 'But I think I have some good news. We have been developing an anti-trauma serum in our laboratories, and the doctors feel that it may be of benefit to your son. It acts directly on the DNA of people affected by shock.'

That's rubbish, Simon thought. But Mrs Hunter obviously didn't know that. She gabbled again, and the Director smiled. It was clear that his plan was working. Whatever it was.

He interrupted her before she had finished. 'For the serum to work properly, we need precise details of the accident. I gather that your daughter was present when Lloyd fell down the quarry.'

'No she wasn't!' Simon said.

He should have known better. The Director pressed a button on the desk beside him. It didn't make any sound inside the laboratory, but it must have rung a bell outside, because two men in white coats appeared immediately. Before Simon could say another word, he found a large hand jammed over his mouth.

The Director went on talking smoothly. 'Just bring your daughter up here, the moment she comes home. I will talk to her myself. Yes . . . Yes, I do think it is your son's only chance of recovery.'

He put the phone down and looked round severely at Simon.

'You cannot be permitted to disrupt my plans.' He waved to the men in white coats. 'Silence him.'

One of the men took off his tie and pulled it tightly round Simon's mouth, gagging him. It dug in painfully, making it hard to breathe.

But that wasn't the worst part. The worst thing was the lizard-girl's face. All the time he was being gagged, he could see her watching him. And there was absolutely no expression on her face. He might just as well have been a wardrobe.

Dinah ran in through the kitchen door—and met a row of eyes. Harvey and Mandy. Ian and Ingrid. And Mrs Hunter—looking stern and cold, as Dinah had never seen her look before. There was a plate full of sandwiches on the table, but it was obvious that nobody felt much like eating.

'At last!' said Ingrid. 'Where have you been, Di?'

'I don't care where she's been,' Mrs Hunter said icily. 'And there's no time to waste on explanations. We've got to get to the BRC, as fast as we can.'

'What?' Dinah caught her breath.

'No argument!' said Mrs Hunter. 'It's not much to ask.' She looked bitterly at Dinah. 'Your father's on his way home. He's resigned from his job because they wouldn't let him come back to see Lloyd. So don't you dare make a fuss about a little thing like going to the BRC.'

'But . . . why?' Dinah said.

Mrs Hunter stood up. 'I'll explain on the way. You'd know already if you'd come to the hospital like everyone else. Instead of refusing to help Lloyd.'

'Instead of *what?*' Dinah stared. 'I didn't refuse to help Lloyd. What are you talking about?'

'You did refuse,' Harvey said heavily. 'I heard you. I phoned up to tell you that the doctors wanted you—and you said you were too busy *collecting evidence.*'

'No I didn't—' Dinah began.

And then she realized that she had said it. Only she'd thought she was speaking to Simon. She sat down suddenly beside Harvey.

'That was *you* on the phone?'

'Of course it was,' Mrs Hunter said impatiently. 'But that's all ancient history now. We can't go back to the hospital. We've got to get to the BRC. They want you there. Urgently.'

You've got to come here. It's urgent. Dinah went cold. The Headmaster was still trying to get her to go to the BRC, was he? What did he want?

'Why me?' she said, in a small voice.

'Because you can tell them exactly what happened when Lloyd fell down the quarry.'

'No I can't!' Dinah looked round wildly. 'I told you all! I never went to the quarry that night!'

The others avoided her eyes, and Mrs Hunter sighed.

'I think we've had enough lies. Why don't you think about Lloyd for a change? If you tell the truth, we might be able to save him.'

'But—'

'I'm going to fetch my coat.'

Miserably, Dinah watched her mother walk out of the kitchen. It was the worst moment of her life. No one believed her. She felt like screaming and bursting into tears.

But that wouldn't help Lloyd. The only thing that would help Lloyd was getting the others to listen to her. And she only had a few seconds to do that, before she was dragged off to the BRC.

She took a deep breath and made herself speak quietly and calmly.

'Look—you all know me. Better than anyone else in the world does. Please listen to me properly, just once.'

Harvey's face stayed wooden and angry, but Mandy wavered.

'We-ell—I suppose it's only fair to listen.'

'Thanks.' Quickly, Dinah pulled Simon's net out of her jacket. 'I wasn't here, because I went to fetch this. It's an insect trap that Simon made—and it's been chewed by something. Something huge.'

'Oh come on—' Ian began.

'Just *look* at it!' Dinah said fiercely. 'I don't know what got caught in here, but I know that there's some kind of

114

monster at the BRC. Something they've produced by genetic engineering—like that creeper.'

'What for?' Ingrid said. 'Why would scientists waste their time making monsters?'

'I don't know why. But I know *who*. He's taken over at the BRC. He got us to come here, by offering Dad a job. And now he's persuaded Mum to take me up to the laboratories.'

'Who?' Mandy said softly.

Dinah took a deep breath. 'The Headmaster!'

'*What?*'

Suddenly, they were all looking at her. But it was too late. Mrs Hunter was already coming back down the stairs.

Dinah spoke as fast as she could. 'I didn't know it was you on the phone, Harvey. Rose said it was Simon. He's trapped in the BRC, and he was trying to get me to go there too. The Headmaster's hypnotized him.'

They were starting to look confused, but Dinah couldn't stop. She had to tell them as much as she could.

'Rose is working for the Headmaster. I saw her let herself into the BRC—with a remote control. It opens a secret door opposite that big oak tree—'

Mrs Hunter came into the kitchen, with the car keys in her hand.

'That's enough, Dinah,' she said coldly. 'I don't know what you're shouting about, but it can wait until we get back. Come on.'

Putting a hand on Dinah's shoulder, she ushered her out of the house.

'You've got to believe me!' Dinah called back, over her shoulder. 'It's Lloyd's only chance.'

But she didn't think they would. She didn't think anyone could believe anything so weird. For a moment she wondered if it was worth trying to tell her mother, but Mrs Hunter was like someone in a daze, just concentrating on getting Dinah to the BRC. Glancing up at her stern, unhappy face, Dinah sank into silence. She didn't think Mrs Hunter would even hear if she tried to explain.

Left alone in the kitchen, the other four looked at each other.

'What do you think?' Ingrid said.

Harvey picked up the net and spread it on the table. 'She's right about this being weird. But . . . *giant insects*?'

Ian looked thoughtful. 'Remember what Di said? About the wood that was chewed? That's what wasps do. I told you before.'

Harvey tried to make sense of it all. 'So what have we got? There's the net. And the chewed wood. And Simon's photos of the creeper—if they're not faked.'

'There's something else,' Mandy said suddenly. 'Hang on.'

She went out into the hall. When she came back, she was holding a letter in a stiff, white envelope.

'This came for Dinah, but there wasn't time to give it to her. It says UNIVERSITY OF WESSEX on the front. Do you think—?'

Harvey snatched the envelope and ripped it open. The others crowded round to read the letter over his shoulder.

Biogenetics Department,
University of Wessex.

Dear Simon James and Dinah Hunter,

Thank you very much indeed for the sample of creeper you sent me. I have done a DNA scan, and there's no doubt that it is a very strange plant indeed.

It would be possible, in my judgement, for a plant like that to evolve, but I estimate that it would take several millions of years, at least, for it to develop from anything now known.

I should be most interested to know where you obtained the sample.

Yours sincerely,
C. Rowe
Professor.

For a moment, no one spoke. Then Ian gave a long, low whistle. 'Maybe it's all true. Let's go up to the hospital. To see if Dinah's right about Lloyd and the buzzing. If that wakes him up—'

'What buzzing?' said a sharp voice from the doorway.

They spun round. Rose was standing in the kitchen doorway, staring at them. For a second, everyone was speechless.

Then Ingrid moved. Suddenly, without any warning, she darted across the kitchen. In one swift movement, she plunged both her hands into Rose's coat pockets.

'Get off!'

Rose tried to pull away, but she was too late. Ingrid sprang back, raising her hand in triumph. She was holding a small piece of black plastic.

'Di was telling the truth about this, anyway! She said Rose had a remote control to get into the BRC—and here it is!'

'Don't be stupid,' Rose said quickly. She snatched it back. 'That's the remote control for our garage door. At home.'

'Really?' Harvey murmured. 'Well, there's an easy way to find out.'

'What do you mean?' Rose glared.

'I'm not going up to the hospital with the others. I'm going to the BRC, with you. To test that thing.'

'Oh yes?' Rose took a step backwards. 'How are you going to make me do that?'

'Like this!' Ingrid said. She clamped her fingers round Rose's right arm. 'I'll come with you, Harvey. So she doesn't get away.'

'Right.' Harvey grabbed Rose's other arm. 'Let's settle this thing, once and for all.'

Chapter 15

Into the Tunnels

Dinah was shaking as she and her mother walked into the BRC.

Mrs Hunter explained who they were and sat down opposite the reception desk, twisting her hands in her lap.

'You will co-operate, won't you?' she whispered. 'And tell them anything that might help?'

'Of course I will,' Dinah whispered back.

Inside her head, a voice was shrieking. *What about me? Maybe I'm in worse danger than Lloyd!* But she wouldn't let it shriek out loud. She made herself look quiet and obedient.

A woman in a white coat came walking down the corridor. 'Dinah Hunter?' she said crisply. 'To see the Director?'

'That's right.' Mrs Hunter stood up.

'There is no need for you to come.' The woman's voice was brisk and mechanical. 'You will stay here.'

She raised a hand, signalling to the receptionist, and a cup of coffee appeared, as if from nowhere. Mrs Hunter took it, looking confused.

'I . . . it's very nice of you, but . . . I think I ought to—'

'You will stay here,' the woman in the white coat said again.

Dinah tried not to look as nervous as she felt. 'Don't worry, Mum. I'll be fine.'

Mrs Hunter sat down, and the woman whisked Dinah away down a long, bare corridor, not making any attempt to talk or smile. When they reached the Director's office, she knocked on the door.

'Dinah Hunter to see the Director,' she said into the intercom.

There was no answer. The door simply swung open.

'You may enter,' the woman said, stepping back to let Dinah go in on her own.

Dinah stepped over the threshold and the door swung shut behind her. For a second she was alone in the orderly, grey office. Then another door opened in the opposite wall.

'Good afternoon,' said a precise, expressionless voice.

Even though she had guessed who he was, it was still a shock to see him in the doorway. The Director. The Demon Headmaster. He was standing very still, facing her across the room, and the dark glasses made two pools of shadow in the middle of his narrow, pale face.

'What do you want?' Dinah said.

He raised one eyebrow. 'I was under the impression that it was you who wanted something. Perhaps I am wrong. Perhaps you do not care about Lloyd Hunter.'

'Of course I care about him!' Dinah glared at him. 'But I don't believe all that stuff about anti-trauma serum. It's a load of nonsense.'

The Director looked oddly pleased. 'Your brain is still working well. Excellent. You will need all your mental powers for the challenge I have in mind.'

Dinah looked warily at him. 'What challenge?'

A small smile flitted across his face. 'I am going to give you a chance to save Lloyd Hunter. By identifying the thing that caused his coma.'

Everything inside Dinah's head went very still. 'What have I got to do?'

'That is for you to discover. I am merely giving you the opportunity.'

'What do you mean?'

'You may think you know what kind of creature attacked your brother, but who will believe you? No one will take any notice—unless you can prove it. And there is only one certain way to prove the identity of a living creature.'

Dinah took a long, shaky breath. 'DNA,' she whispered.

'Precisely. Do what I tell you, and you will be able to obtain a sample of the creature's DNA.'

Dinah's heart gave one great, joyful leap. Then her brain began to work. 'But why? *You* don't care about Lloyd.'

The smile vanished. 'You do not need to know why. All you have to do is decide whether you will accept my challenge.'

It was like being blindfolded. She was being challenged, but she hadn't been given any information. Wildly she looked round, but there were no clues in the Director's office. Only an empty desk and a blank computer screen. How could she decide?

And yet—how could she refuse?

She took a deep breath. 'If there's anything I can do to help Lloyd, of course I'll do it.'

The Director nodded. 'That is not a rational decision, but it is the one I expected. Come into the laboratory and I will explain what you have to do.'

He opened the door behind him, beckoning Dinah through. Feeling cold and afraid, she walked across the office and took one step into the room beyond.

Then she stopped dead.

On one side of the lab was a group of technicians in white coats. And right next to them was Simon.

Strapped to a chair and gagged.

Simon was horrified when he saw Dinah walk in. He had never felt more helpless in his life. He wanted to warn her about the Director's DNA experiments. And the way he'd speeded up growth. And the lizard-girl, who was hidden away in another room.

But he couldn't speak a word.

Dinah looked just as horrified. She spun round to the Director.

'Why is Simon tied up like that? Let him go!'

'What I do with intruders is none of your business,' the Director said coldly. 'He is fortunate that I have been so lenient.' He marched across the laboratory and flung open the door on the other side. '*This* is what I brought you to see.'

It was the door where Simon had been captured, coming along the corridor from the secret entrance. But the Director wasn't pointing to the corridor. He was pointing to the steps that went down into darkness. Leading to the underground tunnels.

'Somewhere in those tunnels,' he said softly, 'is what you are looking for. The creature which escaped so . . . unfortunately and attacked your brother.'

'The monster!' Dinah said fiercely.

She was very pale, but she didn't sound frightened. If it hadn't been for his gag, Simon would have cheered.

The Director looked scornful. '*Monster* is a stupid, emotive word. The creature down there is a scientific experiment. One stage in my plan to take charge of nature.'

He did not give Dinah time to ask what he meant. Reaching out, he took a torch from a shelf beside the door. Then he waved towards the dark steps.

'The answer to Lloyd's problem lies down there. All you have to do is find it. And come safely out of the tunnels again.' He held out the torch.

Dinah took a step backwards. 'Is that all you're going to tell me?'

'That is all. If you want to know anything else, you must discover it for yourself.' His eyes were invisible behind the dark glasses. 'You will need to use all your wits, Dinah Hunter. If this really matters to you.'

'Of course it matters.' Dinah lifted her head determinedly. 'I just want to get everything straight. Do you promise to let me go when I come out with this DNA sample?'

The Director gave a small nod. 'That is one of the conditions of the experiment.'

'What about Simon? You've got to let him go too.'

'Simon?' The Director looked startled. 'Simon is irrelevant.'

'He's not irrelevant to me. He's my friend.' Dinah stood stubbornly in the doorway, refusing to take the torch.

Unexpectedly, the Director wavered. Simon saw him glance down at his watch. He frowned, as if he were worried about the time. Dinah stood her ground and, after another moment, he nodded.

'Very well. That can be part of the bargain. It will make it even more urgent for you to succeed.'

He held out the torch again and this time Dinah took it and switched it on. It gave a dull, red light.

She hesitated and glanced round at Simon. He knew what she was thinking.

'You have no choice,' murmured the Director. 'Without a torch, you will be in complete darkness.'

Dinah swallowed. Then she gave Simon a small, nervous smile and walked through the door. He heard the sound of her feet padding down the broken brick steps.

But he didn't hear them for long. The Director shut the door behind her and turned to the technicians.

'Fetch Eve,' he said.

When Eve walked into the laboratory, the Director

didn't waste time greeting her. He simply opened the door again and pointed at the steps.

'Down there is a maze of tunnels. There is an intruder in the tunnels. I want you to follow, and make sure that intruder does not get out. Is that clear? *No one* is to get out of those tunnels.'

'That is clear,' Eve said. 'How do you wish me to prevent the intruder from leaving?'

Her flat, expressionless voice was the most frightening thing that Simon had ever heard. He held his breath.

'You must discover that for yourself,' the Director said. 'You may use any weapon you can find.'

Eve didn't look surprised or worried. Her face didn't change at all. She simply stepped forward, to the top of the steps.

The Director took down a second torch and handed it to her. She switched it on and Simon saw that it was red, like Dinah's.

For one, eerie moment, he felt as if he'd jumped back in time. A couple of minutes before, it had been Dinah standing at the top of those steps. Now it was Eve. Her scaly hand was hidden, and the scaly side of her face was turned away. Standing there, with the red torch, she looked exactly like Dinah.

But she didn't look round and smile, the way Dinah had. She went steadily down the steps, without a backward glance at Simon.

The Director closed the door behind her. Then he turned to the computer and said, 'Activate. Surveillance. System.'

The computer screen fizzed into life, and Simon found

himself staring at a picture. The screen showed a round, brick tunnel, lit by a red light. At the far end of the tunnel was a crouching figure, examining something on the ground. For a second, Simon wasn't sure who it was. Then the figure straightened, facing almost directly into the camera, and he saw that it was Dinah.

She began to walk away down the tunnel, leaving behind whatever it was that she had been looking at.

With a sinking heart, Simon saw the Director smile.

'Mistake Number One, Miss Dinah Hunter.'

At that very moment, Harvey and Ingrid were standing out in the lane with Rose, staring at a blank brick wall.

'Go on,' said Harvey. 'Press the remote control.' But his voice was uncertain.

'You're being ridiculous,' Rose said. 'You'd believe any nonsense if your precious Dinah said it was true. Of course there isn't a door here.'

Harvey did feel ridiculous. But Rose's voice made him more determined. He'd listened to that sneering, sneaky voice too much already. He wasn't going to let it trick him again.

'Press the remote control!' he said fiercely.

Ingrid glowered too and, reluctantly, Rose raised her hand and pressed.

Immediately, a section of wall swung back, and the three of them were looking down steps into a dark cellar. Harvey swallowed and pulled out the torch he'd snatched away from Dinah that morning.

'Come on. We're going to see what's down there.'

Rose stepped back abruptly. 'No,' she said. Her voice

was shaking. 'I'll go along the corridor, but I'm not going down—'

'Yes, you are!' Ingrid said fiercely. She grabbed one of Rose's arms. 'We're all going. Turn the torch on, Harvey.'

Harvey pressed the switch. The torch gave only a dim, red light, but that couldn't be helped. They'd have to make do with it. Harvey caught hold of Rose's other arm and together he and Ingrid pulled her through the door and on to the flight of steps.

They were half-way down the steps when there was a flicker of red light ahead of them. A figure in a track suit darted suddenly across the far end of the tunnel, following another passage and shining a red torch to light her way.

'Dinah!' shouted Ingrid.

Harvey was just as startled. Letting go of Rose's arm, he ran down the steps. 'Di! Stop!'

He didn't realize that Ingrid had let go as well. He was too busy yelling after the figure that had vanished down the other tunnel. He didn't see Rose sneaking away up the steps. Not until he heard her feet at the top.

He and Ingrid spun round, but it was too late. Rose stood silhouetted in the doorway, raising her hand triumphantly to press the remote control.

Then she disappeared, as the door swung shut in front of her, cutting off all the light except the red glow from the torch.

They were trapped.

Chapter 16

No Exit

Dinah was much further ahead, deep in the maze of tunnels. She was following the buzzing.

She had caught the sound of it, very faintly, when she was crouching in the first tunnel, examining some of the little brown seed pods from the creeper. She was trying to work out what they were doing there, on the earthy floor, when she heard—

Bzzz-ZZZ-zzz-ZZZ.

The noise drove the seed pods out of her mind. That buzzing was the key to the whole problem. If she could prove what was buzzing, she would know what had given Lloyd the massive, dreadful shock.

The thought of what she might find made her tremble, but she didn't let it put her off. Slowly she inched along the tunnels. Whenever she had to make a turn, she listened carefully and chose the turn where the buzzing sounded loudest.

It couldn't be far now. She had been moving in roughly the same direction all the time. She must be very near the ice house.

The Director was smiling. Simon shivered to see how pleased he looked as he stared at the screen.

It had divided into two sections. In the left hand one was Dinah, slowly feeling her way along the damp brick tunnels. Every time she came to a junction, she stopped and tilted her head, as if she were listening. Simon couldn't hear the sound, but he had a pretty good idea what she was listening for.

On the other side of the screen was Eve, moving faster, but creeping more quietly. She was holding something in her hand. From time to time, she stopped and crouched down, poking with her fingers at the earth floor of the tunnel.

At first, Simon didn't realize what she was doing. Then, the third or fourth time she stopped, he managed to see what she was holding. She had a handful of seed pods from the creeper and every time she stopped, she was planting some of the seeds in the floor of the tunnel.

Simon went cold. Red light and creeper seeds.

In his mind, he could see the long shoots of the creeper poking their tips through the earth. Sensing the red light ahead of them. Slithering along the tunnels as they grew.

He hadn't noticed the Director turning to look at him. Not until he spoke.

'You see? Eve is more rational than Dinah Hunter. Her wits are sharper. *She* has guessed that the seeds were put there specially, to be used. Do you want to see what she is doing?' He raised his voice and spoke to the computer. 'Display. Tunnel. Diagram.'

The picture on the screen changed. Dinah and Eve both disappeared and Simon found himself looking at a map which showed half a web of interlacing tunnels. They all led towards a round space. The ice house.

But the picture wasn't simply a map. It was moving and changing all the time. The Director waved a hand, pointing at one of the wide tunnels. It was gradually turning green from one end to the other.

'My sensors are picking up oxygen from the creeper,' he murmured. 'Look how fast it grows. Each generation is quicker than the last.'

His hand waved again and again, and Simon saw that the green was stealing up other tunnels as well. The creeper was growing almost as fast as Dinah was walking. And it was blocking one tunnel after another.

'She will not escape,' the Director said, with satisfaction. He pointed to a small red dot, inching along one of the tunnels. 'There is Dinah's torch. She is almost trapped already. Even if she discovers what she wants to know, she will not be able to get out again. Before then, Eve will have closed off all the escape routes. See how busy she is.'

He pointed at another red dot. Eve's torch. Simon could tell that Eve wasn't following Dinah. She was darting round the web of tunnels, planting her seeds.

Struggling at the straps, Simon grunted fiercely behind his gag. He felt powerless and desperate. He had no way of interfering with the Director's plans. All he could do was watch helplessly while Dinah was trapped by the creepers.

Suddenly, the Director's face changed. He took a sharp step forward, peering at the computer screen. Simon leaned forward too, to see what had caught his eye. It was a third red dot, near the side of the map. Moving in towards the middle.

Spinning round, the Director barked at the technicians. 'Go out to the secret door. See if it has been tampered with. Someone has come in that way. There is another torch.'

The technicians slid out immediately, into the office. The Director turned back to the screen. 'Display. Area. Fourteen.'

When the picture appeared on the screen, Simon could hardly believe his eyes. There was Harvey, walking down one of the tunnels, with a girl close behind him.

It was Ingrid who saw the creeper first. As they crossed another tunnel, she looked left, and clutched at the back of Harvey's sweatshirt.

'Look!'

Harvey spun round, aiming the torch where she pointed. The whole of the left hand tunnel was crammed with long, tangled shoots of creeper, as thick as brambles. The moment the red light hit them, they began to move, untangling themselves and slithering over the floor of the tunnel towards the torch.

Harvey couldn't believe his eyes. 'That's impossible.'

'It's not impossible!' Ingrid gulped. 'It's happening. Quick!'

She tugged at Harvey's sleeve, pulling him on down the tunnel ahead. But they didn't get far. In a few yards the main tunnel was blocked by creeper. That was slithering towards them too.

'We ought to get out of here!' Harvey said desperately. 'Let's go back and break down the secret door.'

They spun round—and saw that there was no chance of going back. The creeper behind had followed them.

'Look! We'll have to go this way!' Ingrid gasped. She turned right, into a much narrower tunnel. 'Come on!'

'Wait a minute!' Something was nagging at the back of Harvey's brain. 'What was it Dinah said? About those creepers she grew?'

'Of course!' Ingrid yelled. 'They followed the light. Drop the torch, Harvey. That's what's making them follow us.'

Harvey hesitated. 'We'll be in the dark.'

'That's better than being strangled by creepers. Come on!'

Harvey left the torch on, to distract the creepers, and put it down on the floor. Then he followed Ingrid into the side tunnel. When they glanced back, they saw the creepers snaking slowly into view, heading for the red light. They met on top of the torch and knotted round it, twisting tightly together. Tighter and tighter.

Ingrid shivered. 'It's horrible. Is that what they would have done to us, if we'd still had the torch?'

'I think so. And you know what that means.'

Ingrid nodded fiercely. 'We've got to find Di! That torch she had was red too.'

Unsteadily, the two of them felt their way round a bend and on down the dark tunnel.

The buzzing was so loud now that Dinah was almost deafened by it. Ahead of her she could see the tunnel opening out into a wider, higher space.

The ice house!

She almost ran the last few metres, tumbling out of the tunnel and looking up, towards the noise.

For a moment, she couldn't grasp what she was seeing. The ice house rose above her in a huge brick dome and on each side of her staircases curved away, rising up the walls. One ran round the left side of the dome and one round the right.

They met on the far side, near the top, at the ice house door. Dinah caught a glimpse of the rotten wood of the door, with the hole gnawed in it. But most of the light from the hole was blocked out by a great pale shape hanging from the ceiling. A vast globe, as big as a car.

That was where the buzzing was coming from.

Dinah stepped forward. Slowly she stood on tiptoe and raised an arm. She could just reach the bottom of the globe and she stretched out and touched its rough, papery surface. It felt like chewed wood.

As her fingers brushed against it, the buzzing stopped. And Dinah heard another noise that froze the breath in her throat.

There was something moving round inside the globe. Something big.

Chapter 17

In the Ice House

Simon could see it too. The screen in the lab showed the whole of the great pale globe, and the shadow of the thing that was moving inside it. He clutched at the arms of his chair.

It was a wasp's nest. He recognized the shape, and the way it hung from the ceiling. And he could imagine the great queen wasp inside, getting ready to lay her eggs. If he had been in Dinah's place, he would have run away.

He did see her hesitate for a moment as she stared up. But she didn't run. She squared her shoulders and began to climb one of the flights of stairs that curved up the ice house wall. To get closer to the nest.

Simon's heart thudded. If it hadn't been for the gag, he would have yelled out useless warnings. She was going to get killed, he knew it. The wasp was going to sting her.

Just as it must have stung Lloyd!

Dinah was still climbing the steps when the door from the office into the lab was suddenly flung wide open. The Director turned round, looking irritated.

'I do not wish to be disturbed—' he began. But then he saw who was coming in. It was Rose, between two technicians. 'What are you doing here?' he snapped.

Rose was obviously nervous, because she began to gabble. 'I did the best I could, sir. Dinah's friends found out I was working for you. It wasn't my fault. They guessed, and—'

The Director raised a hand. 'Don't talk to me about *fault*. I will decide whose fault it is. Just tell me what has happened.'

Rose twisted her hands together. 'Two of them went to the hospital, to try and wake Lloyd up. Something about buzzing. And the other two—'

'I know where they are,' the Director interrupted sourly. 'You let them in by the secret door. Even though I had told you to show no one that entrance.'

'They made me!' Rose was gabbling again. 'But they won't get out again. They've gone down to the ice house. I thought—'

'I don't care what you thought,' the Director said witheringly. 'You have interfered with my plans. Go and stand over there, beside Simon. I will deal with you later.'

Rose obeyed, without any hesitation, but Simon could see that she was trembling. Avoiding his eyes, she stood beside his chair, looking white and shaken.

The Director had turned back towards the screen, watching closely. For a second, Simon couldn't work out what had caught his attention. Then he saw. Eve had appeared in the ice house. She was moving round it, making sure that the wasp's nest kept her hidden from Dinah. And, as she went, she was sowing seeds in every tunnel entrance.

By the time she sowed the last seeds, shoots were already poking out of the earth in the first entrance. Eve gave them a quick, satisfied glance and then began to climb the second flight of steps, opposite Dinah's.

Half-way up, she passed another entrance, high in the wall of the ice house. Simon saw her hesitate, fingering the

135

seeds she was holding. But there was no earth there for them to grow in, and she moved on without dropping any.

The camera that was filming her was at the top of those stairs. Simon watched the top of her head getting closer and closer as she climbed towards it. Finally, she crouched down to hide immediately underneath it. Invisible from everywhere else in the ice house.

She was just in time. As she hid herself, Harvey and Ingrid came out into the ice house, fighting their way through the creeper that was growing across the tunnel entrance.

'Di!' Harvey called. 'It's us!'

Dinah almost fell off the stairs when she saw Harvey and Ingrid. 'How on earth—?'

'Never mind that!' Ingrid shouted, above the buzzing. 'You've got to get out of here. The place is full of creeper!'

Dinah looked down and saw it for the first time. Long, green shoots snaking up the tunnels. Spiralling into tight tangles, to block the way out.

'It's all right,' she called back. 'There's a door up here. We can get out that way, into the garden and over the wall into the woods. But not yet. I've got to get a DNA sample, to prove what attacked Lloyd.'

She thought Harvey would argue, the way he'd been arguing ever since Lloyd's accident. But he didn't.

All he said was, 'What can we do to help?'

Dinah looked at the nest. 'Nothing yet. Let me try and lure this . . . this *thing* out of the nest.'

'You think you can?' Ingrid said.

'Maybe if I touch the nest?' Dinah reached out nervously. This time, when she touched the papery surface, the buzzing grew louder and fiercer. Automatically, she shrank back against the wall. As she did so, she felt a lump digging into her side. For a second, she couldn't think what it was. And then she remembered.

The treacle!

That was the way to lure the thing out of its nest. Frantically, she dug her fingers under the rim of the lid to lever it off. Scooping out the treacle, she began to smear it on to the ice house wall, as close to the nest as she could.

'Hurry up!' yelled Harvey. 'The creeper's growing fast!'

Dinah glanced down, and caught her breath. All the exits on the ground were blocked now, and the creeper was beginning to cover the floor. Harvey and Ingrid were inching towards the steps.

'Don't come up here!' Dinah called. 'It might be dangerous. Go up the other steps. They meet these at the top. By the door.'

The buzzing was getting frantic now. She had thought the creature would come out of its nest at the bottom, but it was scraping and clawing at the side of the nest, trying to get straight through to the treacle. Dinah cowered back against the wall. *I mustn't run away*, she was saying to herself, over and over again. *This is the only chance to save Lloyd. I mustn't run away . . .*

Simon couldn't believe she was still there. He was even more frightened than she was, because he knew something that she didn't.

She wasn't going to have an easy time getting through the door at the top of the stairs. Because Eve was up there, ready to stop her.

How was she planning to do it? Simon looked over at the other half of the screen, to see what Eve was up to.

But, just at that moment, the picture on the right hand side of the screen vanished. The image fizzed and disappeared completely, leaving a blank. With an angry mutter, the Director stepped forward and began tapping at the computer keyboard.

There was a little whimper beside Simon. 'Oh, sir. Please, sir . . .'

He glanced up at Rose—and saw that she was utterly terrified. Her face was chalk-white now and she sounded as if she were choking. *She's scared out of her wits*, Simon thought. *Paralysed. Why? Because of that thing inside the nest?*

'Please, sir . . .'

The Director didn't even look round. 'Silence!' he muttered. 'Can't you see that I'm busy?'

Rose's eyes were glazed, and she was staring at the screen as if her worst nightmare was about to appear.

It's your own fault! Simon thought. *Can't you see?* He wished he could tell her straight out. But he couldn't, so he leaned sideways and nudged at her arm, with his head.

Rose gave a tremendous jump, and suddenly went rigid. Her eyes rolled up in their sockets, showing the whites, as if she were in a trance.

Simon nudged her again, as hard as he could. For a second, he thought she hadn't even felt it. Then she blinked twice. Slowly she looked round, like someone waking out of a long sleep. Simon grunted through his gag and she bent her head and stared down at him. Almost as if she were seeing him for the first time. She looked bewildered and shocked. *Great!* Simon wanted to say. *You finally realized there's something dreadful going on!* But all he could do was nod and pull faces.

Rose bent down, and hissed in his ear. 'Look—I'll untie you. But you've got to help me if that . . . that *thing* from the ice house gets up here.' Her voice was shaking.

Simon nodded harder and, with one eye on the Director, Rose unknotted his gag. She left it looped loosely round his head and began to unbuckle the straps that fixed him to the chair.

The Director was too busy to be aware of them. He was concentrating on the computer. As Rose freed Simon's hands, he stepped back, scanning the screen. Then he gave a satisfied nod.

He had swivelled one of the computer-controlled cameras in the ice house, angling it to get a view of Eve. She was visible from the other side of the ice house now, as a distant figure crouched at the top of a flight of steps.

And it was obvious why the camera over her head wasn't working.

A strand of creeper had grown up the cables that led to the camera, twisting tight. And the wires had broken and shorted. Simon could see wisps of smoke curling up through the middle of the creeper. Its leaves were beginning to smoulder.

Eve was watching the smoke. Fascinated. Her eyes followed it as it spiralled up towards the ceiling. Then they darted back to the creeper, as the first small flame flickered among its shoots. Her right hand reached out, towards the twisted stems.

No! Simon thought. But he heard Rose catch her breath,

and he knew it was no use wishing. Eve—obedient,
emotionless Eve—was going to do the logical thing, to stop
anyone getting out of the ice house.

As calmly as if she were picking flowers, she reached out
for a piece of the burning creeper.

Dinah could smell burning, but she thought she was
imagining it. And she didn't dare to look round, because
the nest was beginning to split. Desperate to get at the
treacle, the wasp was fighting its way out.

Dinah flattened herself against the wall and held her
breath. *I mustn't run away . . .*

With a great crack, the nest burst open, and a head

poked through. A head out of a nightmare, with waving antennae and huge, blank eyes.

Dinah couldn't have moved now, not if she'd wanted to. She was paralysed with fear. She stood, staring in horror, as the giant wasp began to drag itself through the ragged gap it had scraped in the side of the nest, buzzing angrily as it struggled towards the treacle.

Pushing its way out, it snagged a wing on the rough edge of the hole. Impatiently, the wasp wrenched itself forward, and there was a rip. A small piece of wing, the size of Dinah's hand, was left caught on the nest.

Dinah could hardly breathe. *I've got to get that*, she thought desperately. *I've got to make myself move, and get it.*

From the stairs on the other side, Harvey called urgently, 'Hurry! The creeper's coming up the stairs!'

The wasp had reached the treacle, and was beginning to feed. With a huge effort, Dinah inched her hand forward, over its head, and tugged at the piece of wing that had been torn off. It was as thick as heavy polythene, but it came free from the nest and fell into her hand. She stood up and scrambled away from the wasp, up the steps.

'I've done it!' she yelled. 'Let's go!'

Simon heard the yell. And so did Eve. He saw her stand up, with the burning creeper in her hand. Drawing back her arm, she flung it, straight at the hole in the ice house door.

'Excellent,' said the Director. 'The perfect, logical solution.'

There was a thick tangle of dead creeper outside the door. It all went up instantly, in a sheet of flame that shot through the hole, back into the ice house. Fire licked at the side of the wasp's nest, and clouds of smoke began to billow downwards.

Chapter 18

The End of the Experiment?

Harvey didn't know what had happened. He just knew that the whole place had suddenly filled with smoke. Somewhere above his head, he could hear the crackling of flames.

'Di!' he called frantically. 'Are you all right?' He ran further up the steps, peering into the smoke.

There she was. She must have come past the door, where the two staircases joined, because he could see her quite clearly, sitting huddled against the wall above him. She was wearing a strange track suit, and there was smoke curling all round her, but it was Dinah all right.

'Di!' he called.

'Don't go up there!' Ingrid hauled at his arm. 'That's where the fire is. Come down here. There's a tunnel with no creeper in it. We'll have to get out this way.'

'But there's Dinah!' Harvey yelled. 'Look! We can't leave her. Come on, Di!'

Slowly the figure at the top of the stairs stood up. She seemed oddly stiff.

'Quick!' Harvey shouted.

She began to move, but she had only taken a couple of steps when her foot slipped sideways. It crashed through the side of the wasp's nest, trapping her leg. She didn't seem to be able to pull it free.

'I'm coming!' Harvey shouted.

Tugging his arm away from Ingrid, he raced up the steps, into the smoke. Leaning out sideways, he reached for a hand.

'Grab hold of me, Di! I'll pull you out!' Dimly, through the smoke, he saw a hand waving towards him. He snatched at it, clutching it tight.

And then he went cold.

What he was holding wasn't a hand at all. It was a scaly claw. Like a giant lizard's.

'Di?' he said, in horror. He tried to pull free of it, but it wouldn't let go.

Then, from right at the top of the stairs, a voice said, 'I'm here!'

As if he were in a dream, he saw Dinah's face. Again. She had come racing straight through the flames by the door, and her hair was smouldering, but it was Dinah all right. His sister.

And the *thing* he was holding—?

He turned back, and Dinah followed his eyes. For a split second, she froze.

It was like staring into a mirror. Her own face—but not her own. The eyes that stared back at her were as cold as ice. And there were tired wrinkles forming round the eyes.

'Who—?'

Who are you? she was going to say. But the flames crackled again, and she knew they were in terrible danger. Questions would have to wait.

Scrambling down the steps towards Harvey, Dinah tucked the precious piece of wing into her pocket and caught hold of the girl's other hand.

'We've got to get her out. Quick!'

They hauled as hard as they could, choking and spluttering as the smoke curled round them. The smell of scorching was growing stronger all the time, and they could hear the angry buzzing of the monster wasp, still busy with the treacle.

The moment the lizard-girl's legs came free, they raced for the doorway where Ingrid was standing.

'Come on!' she shrieked. 'The whole place is going to go up!'

She wasn't exaggerating. They were only just inside the tunnel when the wasp's nest finally caught fire, with a great belch of flame. Smoke billowed into their tunnel, making it impossible to see anything.

They ran. Eyes streaming, breath coming in raw, desperate gasps, they staggered ahead, dragging the lizard-girl with them.

She seemed to be having trouble walking. Several times she stumbled, and then she began to limp. Dinah and Harvey hooked her arms round their necks and half-carried her.

They had no choice about where to go. Every side entrance was full of creeper, some of it dead and dry and some of it newly sprouted. They had to take the only way they could, and the tunnel led them on, relentlessly, towards the steps where Dinah had come down. The steps up to the laboratory.

'We . . . can't go . . . up there,' Dinah panted. 'The Headmaster's . . . up there.'

The fire was hot on their backs, roaring through the tunnels and lighting everything with a dull red glow. And below the sound of the fire was the rustle of the creeper. Still growing, just ahead of the flames.

'There's no other way out!' Ingrid said. 'We've got to go up there!'

The lizard-girl collapsed sideways, against Dinah's shoulder.

'I can't—' she muttered.

Her voice sounded cracked and shaky.

'You *must!*' said Dinah. 'Come on, Harvey. We'll have to carry her.'

Together, they picked her up and started up the stairs. She seemed strangely light and insubstantial. Ingrid was just ahead of them and when she reached the top, she flung the door wide open.

The Director was standing just inside, looking down at them. For one terrible moment, Dinah thought he was going to slam the door again and lock them in with the flames.

But his eyes were on the lizard-girl.

'Bring her in here,' he said crisply. 'Let me see her.'

Dinah and Harvey carried her up the last few steps and laid her gently on the floor.

When they saw her in the light, they were horrified. She seemed to have shrivelled away. Her skin was grey and wrinkled, and her hair had fallen out, leaving only a few dull wisps.

'She's . . . she's dying,' Dinah said. She spun round to the Director. 'What can you do? Can you save her?'

'Save her?' He looked at Dinah as if she were mad. 'Why should I save a creature like that? Her life is over. Rather sooner than I had expected—'

He glanced down coldly at the lizard-girl. With an enormous effort, she moved her head, raising it just off the floor to gaze back at him. Dinah felt her eyes prick with tears, but the Director was unmoved.

'She has served her purpose,' he said. 'I have gained valuable information from her, but the design needs improving. She ages too fast.'

'Is that all you can say?' Simon jumped out of his chair, throwing aside the straps. 'What about *her*? She hasn't had a chance!'

'Poor thing!' said Rose. She glared at the Director and fell on her knees beside the lizard-girl, stroking her shrunken cheek.

All the others bent over her. Dinah and Harvey. Simon and Ingrid. Eve's eyes slid from one face to another, glazing over as they moved. When they reached Dinah, they stopped. Eve stared at her, as if she were seeing her for the very first time. Then, with a great effort, she raised her hand and a faint smile drifted on to her face.

'Friend,' she whispered, so softly that they could hardly hear.

'Friend,' Dinah said, almost choking. She stretched out her arm and for a second she and Eve clasped hands.

Then, with a little sigh, Eve flopped sideways. And, in front of their eyes, she crumbled into dust. Her flesh withered and shrivelled, like the dry leaves of the creeper. For another second or two, it held its shape. Then it fell away into a soft grey powder.

None of them could speak. They stared down silently at the dust that had been a living creature only moments before. Ingrid caught her breath in a loud sob.

The Director looked disgusted. 'Emotion!' he said, sourly. 'The curse of the human race. You can drool over this creature if you like. I am going to use my time more sensibly, by redesigning her DNA.'

He bent down and scooped up a handful of the dust. Then he strode across to the computer and snapped at it. 'Display. DNA. Of. Experiment.'

A whirling double helix appeared on the screen and he leaned forward, peering closely at it, muttering to himself.

'. . . all it needs is a slight reduction in the ageing factor. Then, at last, my design will be perfect!'

Dinah stared at him, feeling sick. Couldn't anything stop him? Was there nothing they could do?

Harvey nudged her. 'Look!' he whispered.

He pointed backwards, at the door they had just come through. Glancing round, Dinah saw something long and green slithering up the steps.

It was the creeper! The red glow of the fire must have given it an extra vigour, because it was growing faster than the flames could burn it. It snaked into the room, sinister and silent.

At that very moment, the Director straightened.

'Excellent!' he said, staring triumphantly at the screen. 'Now I have made the modifications, the DNA pattern is perfect. All I need to do is feed in this old DNA, to form the basis of the next experiment.'

Leaning forward, he tossed his handful of dust into the big, round hole just below the computer screen. Then he reached up to turn on the switch above.

Immediately, huge letters appeared on the computer
screen.

DNA RECONSTRUCTION ABOUT TO BEGIN
STAND WELL CLEAR

The letters began to flash. Changing from white to red.

Just in time, Dinah realized what was going to happen. She grabbed Harvey, pulling him aside. At the same instant, Simon dragged Ingrid the other way. The creeper came shooting through the gap between them, growing towards the red light on the screen. At incredible speed.

The Director didn't see it, because he was still facing the computer. The shoots hit him in the back, knocking him off his feet.

'No!' Dinah shouted. 'Watch out!'

She flung herself forward, trying to grab his legs. But there was no time. With a yell, the Director tumbled into the chute that gaped in front of him. Before Dinah could reach him, he had vanished down the hole.

She stared after him, white-faced and shaking. There was no yelling now. Only a soft shuffling, scrunching sound.

Simon stared too. '*The chute was designed to cope with any living organism,*' he murmured.

The scrunching stopped, and different letters appeared on the screen, in another burst of red.

NEW DNA RECEIVED
DEVELOP THIS DNA? Y/N

The new light speeded up the creeper. More of it slithered up the stairs and into the lab, heading for the screen. Long shoots curled across the room, twisting round the lizard tank and the computer terminals.

'Let's get out of here!' yelled Harvey. 'Before anything else happens!'

They all raced through the office door and out into the corridor. Two bewildered technicians stared at them as they passed, but no one made any attempt to stop them. Running down the corridor, they burst into reception.

Mrs Hunter leapt to her feet. 'Dinah! At last. What—?'

Then she saw the others and stopped, her eyes widening in amazement.

'Quick!' Dinah said. 'Let's get to the hospital! We know exactly what's wrong with Lloyd now—and we can prove it!'

'Explain again,' Lloyd said. He was sitting up in bed, with all the wires and tubes taken off at last. 'Mandy and Ian woke me up with the buzzing, and Dad came and then you lot raced in—and I missed all the rest.'

'There was no time to waste,' Dinah said. 'The doctors told Mum you were getting worse and worse. You had to have those injections, the moment they were sure what to inject you with.'

'Thanks!' Lloyd pulled a face. 'But what's the *Headmaster* got to do with it all?'

'He was trying to take over evolution,' Harvey said. 'The wasp was one of his experiments.'

'One of his monsters, you mean!' Ingrid pulled a face. 'I'm *glad* he fell into that horrible machine. Especially after what he did to poor Eve.'

'*Poor* Eve?' Mandy looked surprised. 'I thought she tried to kill you?'

'That wasn't her fault,' Dinah said softly. 'It was how he made her. And even then she was all right in the end. Wasn't she, Simon?'

Simon nodded. 'She was more human than he was, if you ask me. I'm glad he's gone.'

'Thanks to SPLAT!' Ian said, triumphantly.

'Thanks to Simon as well,' said Dinah. 'Don't forget him.'

'Of course we won't forget him.' Lloyd levered himself up on to one elbow. 'I know we're going back to our old house, Simon, but we'll keep in touch. How would you like to be an honorary SPLAT member?'

Simon went pink with pleasure. 'That would be wonderful.'

Lloyd beamed at him. 'We'll send you SPLAT newsletters.'

'And have you to stay,' said Harvey.

'And we can all go on SPLAT expeditions in the holidays,' said Mandy.

'And I'll let you know what happens here,' Simon said. 'It's already getting back to normal. Dad actually smiled at Rose when she came round yesterday.'

'Rose came to see you?' Harvey grinned.

Simon went even pinker. 'Well, she and her mum are staying in the village, so she's going to need a friend. And she's OK. Now.'

'Another triumph for SPLAT!' yelled Ian.

Ingrid nodded. Jumping on to Lloyd's bed, she raised both arms in the air. 'Come on, everyone! Let's hear it all over the hospital!'

The shout was so loud that three nurses came to see what was the matter.

'SPLAT for ever!!!!'

Dinah didn't think of the computer screen until she was in bed that night. She was just drifting off to sleep, when she suddenly remembered the letters that had been flashing there, as they all ran out of the lab.

NEW DNA RECEIVED
DEVELOP THIS DNA? Y/N

Suppose someone pressed the Y? she thought muzzily. *Could the creeper shoots do that?*

She was still wondering when she fell asleep.

OTHER TITLES IN THE DEMON HEADMASTER SERIES

The Demon Headmaster
ISBN 0 19 271742 1

On the first day at her new school, Dinah realizes that something is horribly wrong. All the children are too neat and well-behaved, and they never stop working. The prefects act like secret police, and behind it all is the strange, terrifying figure of the Headmaster. Dinah is determined to find out his secret. But what will happen when she looks into the terrible green eyes of the Demon Headmaster?

The Prime Minister's Brain
ISBN 0 19 271743 X

Everyone at school is playing the new computer game, Octopus Dare—but only Dinah is good enough to beat it. Dinah finds she can't stop playing the game, and she forgets who she is when she looks into the whirling eyes of the Octopus-s-s-s. What is happening, and how is the Demon Headmaster involved? And why does he want to get into the Prime Minister's Brain?

The Revenge of the Demon Headmaster
ISBN 0 19 271744 8

Suddenly everyone's mad about Hunky Parker. People are desperate to buy disgusting Hunky T-shirts and pig-swill yoghurt. And they long for a holiday in The Sty where there is sun and swimming one day and skiing the next. But when Dinah and SPLAT try to investigate, they walk straight into the middle of a fiendish plot by their old enemy— and a race against time. Can they find out what is going on? Can they stop the Demon Headmaster before it's too late?